Khafa

The High Priestess

by

Lory La Selva Paduano

ELEVATION
BOOK PUBLISHING

Published by: Elevation Book Publishing
Atlanta, Georgia 30308
www.elevationbookpublishing.com

La Selva Paduano Lory - 1974
Khafa
The High Priestess
p.cm.
ISBN 978-1-943904-04-4 (pbk)
BISAC FIC027050

" Insight from the Author's perspective "

What do we really know of ancient Egypt? For many, the answers lie with archaeologists and Egyptologists who have spent their lives researching, excavating sites, and recording their finds, making headlines the way Howard Carter did in 1922, when he discovered the tomb of the young Pharaoh Tutankhamun and his buried treasures.

What if there were other beliefs about ancient Egypt? What if there were widespread stories about cultural and indigenous civilizations that occupied the land throughout history? There are! Welcome to a story that incorporates two main characters and storylines. History, Khemitology and fiction. Enter a world where the possibilities are infinite, intriguing, and filled with conspiracies. From the teachings of a well-known Khemitian and archeologist, Abde'l Hakim Awyan and his divine intervention on my inspiration, I bring to you "Khafa The High Priestess."

Contents

Chapter 1

"Antediluvian Beliefs & Traditions"

Instead of beginning with a long quote, I will place the story in a visual context as in giving situations, characters, times and places. For example: As the old woman entered the bedroom, the young teen hugged her stuffed unicorn in anticipation of the night's lessons. Grandmother Anta believed her granddaughter should be taught the ancient lessons of her heritage. Carefully, Grandmother sat in the chair next to the bed, and opened the sacred book for the night's reading.

"In the beginning of human existence," Grandmother began, "women were thought to be the sole parents of their children and were always associated with life and the creation of earth as well. Prior to Christianity, the great mother Goddess was highly regarded and worshipped as mother of all, and priestesses were her servants. The mother Goddess was the quintessence of creation. In ancient Egypt, mostly men dominated the work force in the temples; however, the role of High Priestess still did exist. The women were mainly from the upper echelon of society," read Anta to her granddaughter Elizabeth, whom everyone called Liz.

"Grandma," interrupted Liz, "I want to hear more about what the high priestesses did in the temples. Does the book tell all?" asked the curious 10-year-old Liz, who wanted nothing more than to become an archeologist and who loved history and discoveries.

"It does, my love, now lay back on your pillow and listen carefully," said Anta. Liz adjusted her blanket and pillow making herself comfortable as Anta proceeded to narrate once more.

"In ancient Egypt, between (c. 2686 to 1650 BC) women priests usually had healing duties and had to teach the other priestesses how to use herbs, practical spells and incantations. It was always a mystery, and kept secret by the priestesses for fear of their being caught and then being burnt alive like "witches" were. For thousands of years the craft has had this knowledge, a knowledge where today, a wide variety of books have been written for all. The craft has an unbroken tradition dating back to Paleolithic era (approximately 35, 000 years ago), according to Fredric L. Rice at the Skeptic Tank."

"Wow, that is really cool, Grandma. I wonder what those spells did," said Liz, as her eyes danced around like shining stars in the night sky.

"There is more, now hush," responded Anta as she rearranged Liz's blanket.

"Some of the rituals included a ritual for initiation, a ritual for the seasons and rituals for special occasions. An important ritual was one leading the practice of magic and blessings of the harvest. Naturally, this involved the priestess casting a protective circle in which rituals were performed, leading incantations or prayers and closing the circle according to "The Book of Shadows" by Lady Sheba."

"Grandma, did the high priestesses help the Queens of Egypt?" asked the curious Liz.

"Well, you see that's a good question, but a story for another time. Let me continue and no more interrupting!" said Anta with a stern look.

"In history, especially American history, the craft or Wicca was looked upon as demonic or associated with black magic. Nevertheless, Wicca does possess ethics against black magic that also included the 'harm none' law, which means harm someone and it harms us all. Karma is also a part of it. The 'rule of three' means that negative or positive energy sent out comes back three-fold according to Lady Sheba." Anta lifted her head over the book and found Liz fast asleep. She shut the lamp by her bedside table and slowly got up and placed the book on her dresser.

Liz mumbled, "Grandma, I love you," and Anta answered back, "I love you, my little one." She shut the door and walked to the kitchen where Catherine and Justin, Liz's parents, were.

Justin put down his newspaper and pulled up a chair for his mother Anta, as Catherine put down her reading glasses and spoke. "Do you think it's working?"

"Ahhhh, she is special, undeniably so. I'm reading her stories of the high priestesses and their duties, she loves ancient Egypt!" said Anta with a gleam in her eye. Catherine smiled but Justin wasn't so happy with Anta's words and he made it known.

"Mother, please let's focus on the real stories of Egypt and the important work that archeologists do there. It is important for Liz to know the facts." Justin sat back down gathering his composure before Anta spoke in anger. "You, my own flesh and blood, wish to deny the stories and proof that our ancestors taught us?"

Justin interrupted, "Not now, Mother. This isn't the time to go back to the past!" Justin adjusted his reading glasses and flipped the newspaper once more without a care in the world. Anta got up and walked away without words, her heart in a knot by the words of her son.

After her mother-in-law left, Catherine said, "That is totally unfair and uncalled for, Justin. Liz has a right to talk about her traditions and what she believes in!"

"And for what motive? So my child starts believing in it? Next thing you know, she's parading it all over school, where the bullying gets even worse!" exclaimed Justin who was now furious and had recalled some bullying incidents toward Liz in the past. Liz had her glasses stomped on, and her lunches confiscated by thugs.

"Really Justin? She's the smartest girl in her grade and possibly her school. Are you afraid she might teach the bullies something?" yelled Catherine.

Justin looked at the floor in despair. Catherine stated, "I'm going to bed, you can join me when you put that stubborn attitude in the garbage for good. Until then, the couch is your bed."

***

For Liz, grade five was no picnic. The first day of school consisted of dirty looks and name calling. She was a wreck and she longed for Grandma Anta's calming words. Surprisingly, lunch time went off without a hitch. Liz found a tree to sit under which sheltered her skin from the strong rays of the Georgian sun while she ate and read peacefully. In the near distance, Liz could hear shoes brushing up against the clean cut Kentucky bluegrass and making their way closer to where she sat. Fear struck her heart as she removed her reading glasses. She looked up to the stick figure that blocked the sun. "If you're here to steal my lunch," Liz said, "all I have is this…"

The stick figure interrupted her saying. "I'm not here to steal anything. I just wanna sit and chat."

Liz found this particularly odd since this girl was part of the bullying gang. As Liz stared at her in confusion, the girl spoke again. "I know what you're thinking, I needed a change of scenery. Those kids are starting to piss me off."

Liz stared even harder at the skinny girl with hazel eyes, but she saw nothing. "Look, April, I want no trouble. I never hurt anybody, and I just want to be left alone," said Liz as she picked up her book and dismissed April.

April smiled and said, "I want to make peace. I'm not following the gang anymore. It's not what you think."

"Okay, no worries April. I believe you," said Liz. She put her book down and opened her heart to the possibility that maybe April was turning over a new leaf.

"So? Friends?" said April with a sassy smile.

Liz laughed. "Okay!"

After that, the girls sat together for their whole lunch hour, laughing and getting to know each other.

Liz was a beautiful girl with light greenish-brown eyes, and dark black thick hair. Liz was short and thin; her figure was starting to take some shape. Over the summer, her breasts started to swell and her hips had started to take on an hour-glass shape, making her figure look mature beyond her age.

April was a tall girl and thin as loose leaf paper. Everyone called her "Sticks." Her strawberry red hair was past her waist line and everyone always wanted her to have a seat near her in class so they could braid her hair. April lay on the grass, looked up to the sky and invited Liz to join her as she spoke. "You know, you have child bearing hips, I can see them starting to take shape," she complimented confidently.

"Child bearing hips, now that's a first! I'm not hiding, I'm only 10!" said Liz who shrugged off the silly idea.

"Say what you will, some of us become young women faster than others. Personally, I can't wait!" said April as she picked a dandelion from the grass and mercilessly tore out the petals one by one.

"Grandma told me about bleeding and stuff, but I'm not looking forward to that!" replied Liz with disgust in her eye.

"Oh, it's not that bad. I got mine early this summer and couldn't go in the pool for a week," replied April.

"Now that's young, I hope mine holds off a little," replied Liz. The school bell rang and the girls made a run for it back to class.

Before they knew it, the school day was over. April found Liz after school, and they both walked home together, since they both lived in the same neighborhood.

"You walk really fast," said April.

Liz didn't respond. She didn't want to tell April that she was accustomed to walking fast in order to avoid the bullies, like her who sometimes followed her home. April didn't seem to notice how quiet Liz was. Instead, April talked incessantly, and even admitted that her "gang" was mad at her for talking to Liz at lunch.

Once the girls were in front of Liz's house, April stopped talking long enough to say good bye.

Liz watched from her front porch as April skipped and hopped down the road. Liz was happy to finally have made a friend. Last year, her one and only friend throughout elementary, Raquel Smith, had moved to southern Florida, and this broke her heart completely.

It was nice to have a girlfriend in addition to the twins Johnny and Clay Beaverton who lived down the street. Boys were more understanding and nicer, Liz thought, but a girlfriend was invaluable. You could exchange clothes, apply nail polish on each other's toes, and fix each other's hair. Plus, you could whisper secrets to each other about boys.

"Ah Lizzy, there you are. Grandma fixed you a little snack. Mommy and Daddy won't be home 'til late, and supper will be ready at six," said Anta as she held the door open for Liz to make her way inside.

That day was the best. Liz had a wonderful supper with her Grandma, did her homework, and bathed. She was already in her pajamas by the time her parents walked through the door.

"Hey honey," said Catherine and Justin in sync. Liz noticed that Anta had her book in hand ready for their bedtime story.

"Mom, Dad, where have you been?" asked Liz.

"Your mom and I were out for dinner and went shopping for a new car," replied Justin.

Liz's eyes lit up at the sound of a "new car," for this meant that she wouldn't be seen any longer by her classmates or bullies in the rusted, old 1999 Dodge caravan. That old heap had embarrassed her one too many times, which was the reason she began walking to school. Liz thought her life was taking a turn for the better: a new friend and a new car. What else was in store for her? She had no clue, but a smile on her face seemed appropriate for the time being.

Anta said, "Ok, say goodnight to your mommy and daddy now." Liz did just that. She took her time about it.

Anta spoke again. "Elizabeth Hawann! Please, Grandma would like to go to bed soon you know!" Liz ran to her bed, jumped in and put the blanket over her body and grinned.

"Sorry Grandma," she said as she waited for Anta to seat herself. Liz noticed that her grandmother didn't have her usual history book in hand and looked confused a little. Grandma Anta said, "I know what you are thinking, where's the book? Right?" Liz nodded in agreement.

"Well, there is no book tonight, because I will be telling you another story, one that reflects my ancestors' beliefs and traditions, and mine as well." Liz smiled and didn't even bother to ask what those might be; instead she patiently waited for her grandmother to gather her thoughts.

"This story happened long ago, and before I even begin, you must swear to never tell anyone. Not even your father!" said Anta.

"Grandma, that's cheating and lying. What if he finds out?"

"Well then, you are right. We must not cheat and lie to our parents, so I will never tell this story. Good night!" said Anta.

Liz yelled, "Wait, Grandma, okay, well I guess a little wouldn't hurt. I promise, I won't say a word."

Grandma smiled and sat back down.

Chapter 2

"The High Priestess"

"Ancient Khemit was the name used to describe Egypt or the 'black land' and even myself, a descendant of the Khemitians."

"Wow! Grandma, I have never heard of this!" said Liz as her heart raced.

"Of course you haven't, you are only ten years old. Your father had the teachings taught to him when he was thirteen, by my mother Anka, grandpa Aziz, and myself. But, you are smarter than your father, so I will teach you now!" said Anka who winked at Liz, then continued on.

"The name was for the rich, ancient soil that the Nile nourished during its annual flooding each summer. The flooding of the Nile was a glorified event. It was accountable for the profusion of food supplied from rich agriculture and the significance of all things such as fertility. Scholars of the teachings were fascinated by the indications left behind by the urbane civilization that existed in Khemit from 10,000 to 65,000 years or more ago, whose self-awareness echoed deeply with nature, enabling them to develop apparatuses in advance technologies that befog us today. One of those scholars, well, an archeologist and Egyptologist, was Abd'el Hakim Awyan. He and his associates made our culture very happy by educating the world on our beliefs. Many had come forward prior, but were never heard!" Anta paused and Liz began asking questions.

"So, are you saying, that there is more to Egypt than we know? And...are you saying that maybe history is wrong?"

"Indeed, this is what I am saying, but we must never dismiss the work that he has been done or what the archeologists have worked for," replied Anta choosing her words carefully.

"Grandma! Do you know what this means?" said Liz, who now sprung from her bed and reached for her note book. Anta grabbed her.

"No, you must never write this down. Keep it stored in your memory and use it for when the time is right," insisted Anta.

"Okay, Grandma, I won't, but I think Mr. Awyan was a smart man!"

"And why is that?" asked Anta.

"If others tried to come forward before, well they weren't very smart about it, because at least he found a way to make his teachings known," replied Liz.

Anta smiled and then spoke.

"Yes, I see what you mean. He became an archeologist and slowly introduced his teachings," said Anta.

"Well, that's my theory anyway," replied Liz.

"I'm off to sleep now, get some rest. Grandma is tired," said Anta as she rose up from her seat and stood by the open door. She watched as Liz got into her usual, comfortable position.

"By the way, I'm over it, Grandma!"

But Anta was gone.

Liz fell asleep thinking about her new friend. But her dreams were not all peaceful. She dreamed about the death of her dog Ginger, and the mysterious story that Grandma told.

***

Saturday mornings were all about cartoons and eating cereal by the television in her pajamas. As Liz soaked up her last Cheerio in the bowl, Catherine and Justin waved good-bye as they both headed off to work, leaving Liz and Anta to fend for themselves.

The Hawanns owned a computer repair shop where Catherine worked along her husband's side. They were far from wealthy, but business was steady and prosperous. Grandma Anta lived in the guest home out back built by Justin and his contractor friends, but she spent most of her time in the main home.

Before noon, the doorbell rang, and Liz saw Sticks standing on the porch. She looked as if she had been crying. Liz was hesitant to open the door, but Anta yelled, "Lizzy, get the door please."

As Liz opened the door, she noticed that Sticks was out of breath, dirty at the knees with scrapes and cuts on her arms. Blood gushed from a cut above her eyes. "Oh my gosh, Sticks, get in here, what happened?"

Sticks tried to gather her composure but she couldn't help but cry louder. Anta came to the door and took Sticks by the hand. "Come, I will clean that up for you," said Anta.

Both girls followed Anta to the bathroom where Anta cleaned and bandaged the cut above Sticks' eye. "Whatever trouble you are in, please get out of it," said Anta as she pressed harder on the wound.

"But, it wasn't my fault," replied Sticks.

"I don't care. I do not know you or your parents. Lizzy is my granddaughter, and I want nothing happening to her, got it!" said Anta in a stern voice. Sticks nodded.

After Grandma left the bathroom, the girls fled to Liz's room to chat privately. "Spill the beans," said Liz as she shut the door.

"I was outside playing on my roller blades this morning when the "gang" from school came down my street on their bikes. They started pushing me around, made me fall into a ditch and beat me up. They took my roller blades and threatened to kill me if I ever spoke to you again. I got up and fought back, and told them I wasn't gonna stop being your friend ever. That's when they started chasing me. I had no place to go Liz, I'm sorry," said Sticks as more tears rolled down her pale face.

"It's okay, where are they now?" asked Liz as she made her way to the window and looked out.

"Lucky for me, I lost them when I turned the corner. They don't know I'm here," replied Sticks.

"Okay, here's the deal. We have to get you home; your parents will be worried. First we'll clean you up a little better and you can call them directly from here," said the optimistic Liz.

Sticks picked up the phone and pretended to dial. "Mom, I'm at a friend's house from school right behind our house. I'll be home soon, yeah...huh, yep, I'll be there soon, bye." Sticks hung up.

"Now, take off those pants, and I'll lend you a pair. You can't go home looking like a hobo," said Liz.

The girls laughed themselves silly until Anta opened the door to Liz's bedroom and stared at the girls. "You must go home now. I'm sure your parents want to see you." Sticks' eyes grew wide with fear, almost as if the grim reaper had come to claim her soul.

Liz hadn't said a word and wanted Sticks to stay, but Liz wasn't disobedient in any way. She walked Sticks to the door. Sticks thanked them for taking care of her.

***

Monday morning rolled around, and Sticks was nowhere to be found on Crescent Street. Sticks didn't show up for school, and Liz couldn't shake the feeling that Sticks was in some sort of trouble. The day went by slowly. Liz couldn't focus because she kept thinking about Sticks. When the bell rang at 3 p.m., Liz was still in a daze as she walked towards home. Then she saw them!

The gang of bullies walked up to her with smirks on their faces. They surrounded her, blocking all means of escape. "Where's your friend, Sticks?" asked Nelly, the leader of the gang, and the tallest of them all. The others stood with their arms crossed and disgust in their eyes.

"I don't know…please leave me alone," said Liz as she hugged books and looked down at the ground.

"I think you know, but won't tell. Well, we haven't seen her since Friday. Send her a message, would ya? Tell her we want our money back; all twenty dollars she borrowed or I'll start charging interest!" said Nelly.

Liz's eyes grew wide as she rewound the words Nelly had just spoken: "*We haven't seen her since Friday.*" Liz was alarmed, but she simply nodded to the bullies. Lucky enough, they wanted nothing to do with Liz. Liz sighed in relief as they walked away. Then Liz was furious. Sticks had lied to her about the bullies beating her up on Saturday morning. The more she thought of the lie, the faster she walked, walking so fast she found herself on Sticks' porch knocking on Sticks' door.

A man in his late sixties opened the door. He was fat and sweaty; he looked like he hadn't shaved in five years. He had a receding hairline, and his front teeth had all fallen out. He stunk of liquor, adjusting his belt when he finally spoke. "Well, well, what have we here. You are a dish indeed," said the old man.

Liz backed off in disgust and rolled her eyes. "I'm looking for Sticks. Sorry, I mean April," replied Liz.

"April, she ain't here, but you can come on in and wait for her," he said.

Liz's heart was pounding like a drum. She shook her head.

"Now, c'mon, you aren't afraid of a little old man like me, are ya?" he said.

"That's okay, just tell her Liz came by," replied Liz as she ran away as fast as she could. None of this made any sense to Liz: the beating, the lie, the money, everything! Liz vowed to get to the bottom of this, no matter what.

That night Anta visited Liz in her bedroom, however it was not to tell her the story, which disappointed Liz. "I am tired Liz, and I need to sleep. I promise I will tell you this story tomorrow night. I also want to warn you; your friend is not okay. She's in some sort of trouble. Please be careful, you girls are much too young for the bad of this world. Whatever trouble you see or hear, tell Grandma," said Anta and Liz nodded and pretended to go to sleep as Grandma left her room. Liz had a hard time sleeping that night, except this time it wasn't because of Ginger the dog. Her dreams included vivid scenes of April, falling off a cliff. April fell to her death and Liz stood on the top of the cliff crying and gasping for air.

Liz woke from her dream as Grandma Anta came rushing in. "Lizzy, you are having nightmares again?"

Liz sat up, wiped her forehead and dried the tears in her eyes. "Sorry for waking you, Grandma," said Liz.

Grandma sat down to wipe her granddaughter's tears. "It's 11 p.m., It's late and I can't sleep. Do you want to hear some of the story now?"

"Sure, why not? It will probably make me feel a whole lot better," replied Liz.

Grandma Anta sat back and sighed, "Okay, let's begin.

In the year 2530 B.C. Pharaoh Menkaura dies. It is also believed he ruled at a later date, this isn't for sure, but we know of something different. An ancestor came to rule Egypt from the Doggone culture due to the fact that his blood line was broken, and this is why they say he ruled at a later date. A young girl of the age of seventeen came to rule ancient Egypt. As his predecessor, she was to be Pharaoh until a male heir could be produced. The young girl's name was Aketu. She was later erased from the scriptures and no one knows why." Anta paused while Liz's eyes glowed with anticipation for more.

"Aketu had no knowledge of Reign, and she needed help, guidance and blessings. She was introduced to many able hands, yet had never liked any of the advisors. She often threw them out of her chambers, meetings and even her entertainment forums. She loved the arts, and prayed to the Goddesses and Gods. It was clear that she loved her priestesses the most. With them, she found herself comfortable and at ease, 'til one day, an idea struck her like a lightning bolt."

"The high priestess, the maiden of all ceremonies and the head of them all, was of particular interest to Aketu, simply because she was intelligent, beautiful, knowledgeable, fierce in her teachings and able to lead a pack. Her name was Khafa."

"Khafa's husband had passed away at a young age, and she was childless. She was no more than twenty years of age, and their union was nullified by death after only two months of marriage, leaving her widowed and alone in a brutal world. Nevertheless, she had earned this position due to her husband's former status as a high priest. She had served Menkaura the Pharaoh in the last year of his reign, which had earned the couple a great spot by the King and they had been regarded highly."

Anta cleared her voice and continued, "Aketu watched her closely as she sat on her throne. Every move she made was interesting and captivating as she led the younger priestesses in their rituals. Aketu spoke to one of her servants, 'Bring the high priestess to me. I will have words in private.' The servant nodded and walked over to the priestess who was in the middle of her ceremonial prayer. After the servant whispered into Khafa's ear, she immediately found Pharaoh Aketu and bowed at her feet and spoke. 'Your highness, you have asked for me, and I bow before thee.'

"Come, you and I will speak in my chambers alone." Aketu naturally led the way and Khafa followed. Aketu asked Khafa to have a seat on a bench next to her. 'I asked you here because there is something you must do for me. I have watched you closely for weeks now, and I admire your ceremonial prayers. You have a natural ability of rounding up your priestesses in training. You possess substantial poise and beauty, but it is your knowledge and experience of having served my ancestor that I seek.' Aketu paused and Khafa displayed a placid face before the Pharaoh.

"Whatever you ask shall be done," the priestess said. "If you are asking about guidance, I can only be so humble and give you advice," said Khafa.

"*Ahhhh*, yes, advisor! That's what I need, a helping hand, one who will walk beside me, guide me, teach me between the rights and wrongs. With your experience, Egypt will have a powerful Pharaoh. Because of this, we shall prosper, even the poor!" Aketu grew even more excited at the thought and the vision before her.

"Your highness, I assure you I have not much experience in this field. I don't know how to lead a country, perhaps you are mistaken," said Khafa who now bowed her head and looked upon the floor.

"I know it is not uncommon for a high priestess or priest to hold such status, and your job isn't an easy one, but I promise you this will be a rewarding one, as I will allow you to master both. Because there is no one better than you," said Aketu.

Khafa was cornered and afraid of failure. She spoke again. "You are far too kind with your accolades. If it is your wish, then I must try for my Pharaoh," said Khafa.

"Yes, crossing the lines on beliefs and duty, most will not be in accordance, but who are they? After all, I am Pharaoh and I decide!" said Aketu, who crossed her arms and sat herself on her throne with a half-smile and piercing eyes filled with conviction and happiness.

"If it pleases you, I will attend to you tomorrow. For tomorrow will be a new day," said Khafa. The Pharaoh smiled and dismissed Khafa to return to her ceremony. Pharaoh Aketu had a keen eye for what she called perfection. She had refined taste in textiles, exquisite foods, and gorgeous young men who secretly filled the night time hour. She was a beautiful young lady with Egypt at her finger tips. Only time would prove what Khafa was to Egypt."

Anta paused. Liz had fallen asleep once more. Anta had been talking the last two minutes or so to herself and now the clock read midnight and Anta headed for her bed as well.

***

Morning came quickly for Liz as she sprung up from her bed and reached for her clothes that were spread out on her arm chair. Catherine and Anta were in the kitchen, when Liz took her seat at the table.

"Morning, Love," said Catherine. Anta winked at Liz and placed a pancake on her plate. Catherine poured herself a coffee.

"Wow, pancakes on a Tuesday!" said Liz.

Catherine laughed and said, "It sure is, the shop is doing really well, so your dad wanted to buy things we don't normally eat on a week day. He's proud and loves us, now eat up. You have fifteen minutes before you have to leave," said Catherine.

As Liz dug into her pancakes, Catherine picked up the laundry basket and coffee mug.

"Grandma, I fell asleep last night," whispered Liz.

"No need to whisper, my love. Your dad isn't here and your mom doesn't mind about the story and culture," replied Anta. "Well, I'm off. We will continue tonight, Grandma?" asked Liz.

"Of course, now run along and behave!" replied Anta.

Liz ran for the door and shouted, "Good bye!" to her mom.

Catherine shouted back, "Bye! Have a good day. See you later!"

Liz shut the door tightly. When she took her first step off the porch, Sticks was waiting for her. Liz was shocked and tried to avoid Sticks all together. Sticks grew angry and started yelling at the top of her lungs, while Liz proceeded to walk much faster.

"Why are you not talking to me?" Sticks asked as she followed Liz down the street. Liz paid no attention to Sticks and her words. "Some friend you are!" yelled Sticks, who now threw herself on the grass.

Liz stopped and stared down at Sticks. "Get up you baby!" Liz extended a hand and Sticks cried even harder.

"Really! You are in the wrong and now you won't even take my hand. I'm leaving!" said Liz.

"No! Please, I'll tell you everything!" said Sticks.

"I don't know how to help you if you don't speak up. I worry about you," said Liz.

"My parents died when I was nine…in a car crash. The man at the door is Otis, my grandfather. He's Cajun, and a huge arsehole!" said Sticks.

"Wait a minute. The man at the door, you said? How did you know I came by your house?" asked Liz.

Sticks paused for a minute, then said sadly, "Otis passed on the message to me, like you asked."

"I'm sorry Sticks, about your parents, no child deserves that. I guess you should seek someone to talk to about your issues, it would really help!" said Liz.

Sticks wiped away a tear. "I will, all in due time."

***

The weeks before Christmas, Sticks started coming to school more often. She told everyone she was seeing a psychologist and felt happier. Liz was glad for Sticks and noticed that Sticks had begun acting more mature as winter turned into spring.

School was out in late summer, and Grandma Anta had gone back to Egypt. Anta was to return in early July.

One summer morning, Sticks was at the door ringing the doorbell. Grandma wasn't there to answer and Catherine and Justin were in the backyard. The doorbell kept ringing and Liz shouted, "I'm coming, hold on!"

Sticks smiled when Liz opened the door. "So, I turned twelve and you're eleven, so what shall we old hags do!" said Sticks.

Liz laughed and Sticks joined in. "Come, get up lazy bones, can you come to the park?" asked Sticks.

Liz said, "Actually, can you come to the airport with us? We are leaving in ten minutes to pick up Grandma Anta."

Sticks smiled. "Sure, I've never been there! That would be really cool!"

That afternoon was a fun-filled and adventurous one for Sticks, while Liz had already been to the airport more times than she could remember.

That night Grandma Anta unpacked her bags and gave everyone their souvenirs. It was custom for her and always a must. Sticks was reluctant to go home. Liz worried about her. The rest of the summer passed smoothly and Sticks seemed content to spend most of her time hanging out with Liz.

Then during late summer Grandma Anta became sick. Liz was terrified but Grandma Anta just had some bad indigestion. Grandma would be fine. After all, Liz longed for more of the story.

Chapter 3

"Dissipation"

Soon Grandma Anta got better, but it wasn't 'til the second week Liz's sixth grade year that Grandma Anta returned to telling the tale. "You are ready for the rest now? Let's continue where we left off, shall we?"

Once more, Liz tucked herself comfortably under the sheets ready to listen attentively. She stroked her thick black hair and tied it in a ponytail for sleeping.

"Khafa attended to her duty that morning entering the Pharaoh's chambers and bowing before her," Grandma narrated. "Rise my priestess, you shall no longer greet me on bended knees, she said welcoming Khafa to her friendship, and then she spoke again. "You must always look me in the eye; you will treat me as your equal if you are to guide me in every aspect."

Khafa smiled, acknowledging that she understood before she spoke. "It is with pleasure, whatever your heart desires."

"Come and sit by me, our first order of business will be to brush my hair," said Aketu as she handed Khafa a hair brush. Khafa stood over her puzzled as to why the maids hadn't done this for her that morning.

"I am content with you my priestess, but you speak so little, please tell me about you!" said Aketu, inviting Khafa to conversation.

"I am not interesting; I assure you of this much. You are so beautiful, my Pharaoh. what could be more interesting than Egypt or your rule over it?" said the clever Khafa.

Aketu chuckled in a girlish manner and was intrigued but sat still while the priestess arranged her wig and headpiece.

"You are as beautiful as all stars in the night time sky," said Khafa, as she admired the young beauty before her.

Aketu stood up and smiled. "What is the next order of business according to your thoughts, my priestess?" asked Aketu.

"We don't always have to be so formal, but as your adviser, I suggest you visit Egypt and expose yourself to the people. Show them that you are ruler; you cannot hide in these temples forever. You have been Pharaoh for weeks now, and the people have only seen you twice. Mingle with the crowds, extend a helping hand, embrace the people and spread some joy and distribute wheat to the needy," replied Khafa.

Aketu turned and faced the priestess and stared at her without words for some long minutes, but the Pharaoh no longer intimidated Khafa. "You are wise; I now know I have chosen well. You do not disappoint me: you will be my everything now," said Aketu, who grabbed Khafa's hands and held them tightly.

The Pharaoh followed Khafa's advice. She gathered her most trusted guards, advisors and council who had also agreed that she should be politically involved with the country and show a human and nurturing side of her character and reign. Pharaoh Aketu was impulsive, lively, naive and full of energy. The people loved and hated her for it, and often Khafa stood beside her on podiums and guided her on her dialogue and approach toward the citizens.

Months passed and effusive parties were held for the Pharaoh. One in particular was as grand as they came, where the Pharaoh celebrated birthday.

Then the council and Khafa voted on the future of the Pharaoh without her knowledge. Khafa had been a wonderful servant to her Pharaoh, and in Aketu's mind she could no wrong, but Khafa wasn't all that pleased with some of the Pharaoh's behavior around men. There had been no stopping her insatiable appetite for sexual adventure, and there wasn't anything anyone could do. The Pharaoh conducted herself as a man would. She was frowned upon by the council and citizens."

"Wow, Grandma!" exclaimed Liz, interrupting the story. I'm a little young for all this, don't you think?"

"You are, but it's a natural process of life. One day you will come to know love. In ancient times, her age was considered fruit bearing, the right time for reproduction. Many girls were wed at a very early age, so that they could have many children for their Pharaohs. In modern times, most woman have children in their thirties and sometimes late thirties. It's not always the best idea and you will learn this as you get older, my dear," replied Anta.

Liz smiled thinking back to her sex education class just weeks prior and how the whole process of conception was disturbing.

"Anyway," Grandma said, "back to the story. So, the Pharaoh continued her ways. She loved being with men, but that would soon change."

"Grandma, I'm tired," said Liz. So Anta rose and turned on the night light and shut the door, as she whispered, "Pleasant dreams. Liz was soon fast asleep.

***

Sixth grade flew by fast that year, and on most nights Grandma Anta had been too tired to continue her story. Plus, Grandma Anta spent the winter in Egypt, the place of her birth.

That summer Liz and Sticks talked incessantly about middle school as they hung out at pools and parks, rode bikes, and ate ice cream.

Liz's mother had hired a local baby sitter named Cynthia for the summer. Cynthia and Liz visited zoos, festivals and exhibits to occupy their days. Liz spent a lot of time with Sticks and the girls were inseparable. Sticks seemed troubled from time to time, but Liz thought Sticks was still worrying about the bullies.

Liz got up one August morning around ten and wondered how she had slept so long. And, where was Sticks? Sticks had a habit of showing up before nine just about every morning.

Looking out the front door, Liz noticed the whole street was still fast asleep. The twins weren't outside playing their usual morning basketball, and the street seemed like a ghost town. Cynthia was sitting at the table having her coffee and texting.

When Liz walked in to pour herself a bowl of frosted flakes, Cynthia spoke. "Good morning, sleepy head."

"Morning, Cynthia. Mom left early, didn't she?" asked Liz.

"About a half hour ago. Any plans for today? What would you like to do?" asked Cynthia

"Well, I'm not sure. Did Sticks dropped by while I was sleeping?"

"No, sorry." Liz sighed and wondered what was wrong. She would at least finish breakfast and shower. If Sticks didn't come rolling down the street then, Liz planned to stop by her house.

"I just want to check on Sticks, and I'll be right back after I shower. Is that ok?" asked Liz.

"Sure, I'll come with you for a walk, if you like," chimed the enthusiastic Cynthia.

Liz was ready in less than an hour. Together they walked over to Sticks' place. Liz rang the doorbell, but no one came to the door. After five long minutes of waiting a neighbor from across the street spotted the girls waiting at the door. "If you're looking for April, she's not home. Neither is Otis!"

Liz crossed the street to talk to the woman and asked if she had seen Sticks.

The neighbor made sure to look around to see if any other nosey neighbors had been lurking about. "Now you didn't hear this from me, but this morning at around seven an ambulance picked up April. She was hurt badly, and she was unconscious. They brought her out on a stretcher. Otis was picked up by the police.

Liz's eyes widened and Cynthia held her hand over her mouth. "Cynthia, we have to go to the hospital, can you take me? Please!"

Cynthia agreed and the neighbor informed them that April was at the Northside Hospital. Liz and Cynthia got into Cynthia's car and drove off. Once there, Liz ran towards the entrance. Liz was in a state of panic. She had to see if her best friend Sticks was all right.

When Liz finally reached Sticks' room, she found her friend attached to machines with IV's hooked up to her arm. Sticks was still unconscious. It was a sad sight. A tearful Liz sat down beside her and held her hand.

Neither the nurses nor the doctors would tell Liz what happened. Sticks was a minor and for her protection the medical staff withheld information from anyone who wasn't family.

Khafa

Liz was frustrated that no one was coming to claim her. Liz remembered the stories that Sticks told her about not having any cousins or relatives here in America. She did have some family in Europe, but they never communicated. Otis was her last resort.

Liz cried and cried. How coud a 13-year-old girl be left alone in the world? Her heart sank and she knew she had to do something to help out her friend.

"Finally," Cynthia said it was time to leave. Liz couldn't let go of April's hand.

Liz finally gathered her courage and left the hospital with Cynthia. The ride back home was silent; Liz didn't have a thing to say.

That night Cynthia explained all the events of the day to Catherine, while Liz lay in her bed sobbing and unwilling to eat a morsel of food. Catherine walked in, sat in Anta's chair, reached for Liz's hand and held her tight. "I know honey, it hurts, come let me hold you," said Catherine.

Liz fell into the comfort of her mother's arms.

***

Grandma Anta hadn't returned to America that year either, but one afternoon as Liz came barging in from the back yard, weeks after Sticks' incident, she heard her father Justin on the phone with a hospital in Cairo. "Yes, I understand, yes doctor, we will do all we can. We will be there shortly, thank you, good-bye." Justin hung up the phone and turned to Liz, who had been standing there listening.

"Oh Honey you scared me!"

"Who was that?" asked Liz.

"Come sit beside me, we have to talk," said Justin. He sat down and waited for Liz to sit down beside him. Liz knew some more bad news was on the way.

"Grandma is in a coma," said Justin.

Liz sprung up suddenly and yelled, "WHAT!"

"I'm sorry, she was in a car accident on her way to Saqqarah to visit her sister, and they were hit," replied Justin, his eyes filling with tears. Liz began sobbing as she reached for her dad, and they both sobbed together.

No one ate that night. Justin and Catherine typed away for hours on their laptops looking for the fastest flight to Cairo.

Liz sat on the back porch that evening and thought her world was collapsing. She wondered how so many incidents seemed to have been taking place around her. She stole a few quite moments to speak to God. "God, why have you forsaken me? I have no more tears, please heal Grandma and Sticks. They are my life. Please do not take them away from me, I beg you!"

Justin and Catherine walked on to the porch and sat beside Liz. "It's going to be okay Liz, maybe not today or tomorrow, but it will be. They will both be fine, now...we have some news for you. You are going to Egypt with us! Our plane leaves in two days. Maybe our visit might help jog her brain a little and help her to wake up."

Liz was happy and sad all at once.

"What about Sticks? I need to go see her before we leave, can I?" Justin and Catherine looked at each other and agreed that Cynthia would take Liz there in the morning.

Liz packed her bags that night, knowing they planned to leave in two days' time, but it hadn't stopped her from thinking about Sticks.

Catherine brought Liz over to the hospital to see Sticks, but Sticks was still unconscious. The nurse came in and spoke to Liz about her progress. "Now don't you worry; she's made some real great progress, and last night her hands moved. Hopefully, it's a sign that she's coming to!" Liz smiled and thanked her.

The nurse left the room, but Liz couldn't help but wonder what happened, and so she looked around the room for any clues that the nurses may have left behind. There it was, Sticks' folder was on a table by the side of the door. As Liz opened the folder, she heard a voice say, "You don't need to see that."

It was Sticks! She had finally woken up. Liz stopped dead in her tracks and ran over to the bed and hugged Sticks hard, as tears filled both their eyes. "I knew it! I knew it! You're back!" cried Liz as she held Sticks' hands firmly and watched her struggle to stay awake.

26

"I'm happy you are here. I woke up last night for the first time, but they don't know that," said Sticks.

Liz laughed and called her sneaky. "What happened, Sticks, why are you here?" asked Liz.

Sticks sighed and remained silent.

"It's okay if you don't want to talk about it."

"Help me up a little. I'm ready as I'll ever be. Pass me that glass of water. I need to wash my face so I can wake up," said Sticks. Liz was helpful and did as Sticks asked without question. Then Sticks began to speak about the incident. "It's Otis. He's a monster. I'm going away Liz. I overheard them talking, and they said as soon as I wake up, a social worker would come visit and place me in a youth protection home."

Liz was without words and placed her head down in sadness, but Sticks spoke again. "Hey, don't be sad, I'm happy. My nightmare will be over. I can start a new life.

"They said Otis was taken by the police. What did he do to you?" asked Liz.

Sticks sighed once more and looked out the window. "Liz, he's beaten me senseless for years. I'm sorry about all the lies, but I was ashamed. All I ever wanted was to fit in. When Nelly and the gang would bully us, I decided I had enough, enough at home and enough at school!"

"It doesn't matter. What matters is you'll be okay," said Liz.

Sticks wiped away her tears, then asked, "And how about you? How are things?"

"I'm going to Egypt in two days. Grandma Anta is in coma, and the doctors want the family there," replied Liz.

Sticks stared at Liz for some long minutes, deep into her eyes, as if she wanted to say so much, but hadn't dared. "I'm sorry about your grandmother, I guess it's been a rough week for all."

Liz chuckled a little, but Sticks laughed even harder. Before they knew it, they had been silly little girls again.

Then the nurse walked in. "Well, well, well look who's up. Morning princess!" The nurse walked over to the bed and began taking her vital signs and asked Liz to exit the room so she could run more tests on Sticks.

Liz walked out and Sticks winked at her. "Hey, Liz, stick around outside it won't be long. We need to catch up." Liz nodded and joined her mother who was in the waiting room talking on her phone.

That afternoon Liz and Catherine stayed with Sticks and had a great time. When Liz needed to leave, they took an oath of friendship. "I don't know where you'll be, but take my number and mom's cell number. Call me as soon as you're settled, please!" pleaded Liz as she handed Sticks a piece of paper with the numbers written down.

"I will, and we will hang out like we always have," said Sticks as she reached over and hugged Liz tightly. Both girls cried in each other's arms.

Before they left, Catherine left one more word with Sticks. "If you need anything, call. I'll try to help the best way I can." Sticks nodded and thanked them for coming.

That night Liz spoke to God once more and then cried herself to sleep.

***

Liz woke to the sounds of her mother and father ransacking the house for items to pack in their suitcases. "Morning, Liz, breakfast is on the table. Today you are coming with us to work, as there is no baby-sitter available. Eat up, little lady, we leave in an hour," said Justin as he frantically packed his suitcase. The sleepy Liz slowly walked over to the breakfast table, where French toast was waiting for her.

At her parents' workplace, Liz buried herself in books to make the best of being there. She thought about all the wonderful exhibits she would visit in Egypt, and then a thought came to her. She thought about Khemitology and how this was important to Grandma Anta. It was a mystery, a mystery she would dig into deeper and deeper.

Chapter 4

"Over Time"

Visiting Egypt was a beautiful experience for any child to have, especially for a twelve-year-old girl with a vivid imagination. A reconnection with one's roots was always a must at some point in their life. In Egypt, Liz began to broaden her horizons. She felt Egypt was her destiny, the destiny she had imagined since she was a child.

Though Liz had found her destiny, Grandma Anta never woken from her coma. After Liz's parents flew her home from Cairo, she stayed in the guest room in the back of the house. Grandma Anta had care givers and nurses who watched her round the clock. For five long years, Grandma stayed in her coma, and Liz spent most of her high school years hoping for a miracle.

Liz was now seventeen and high school had come and gone. Sticks never called Liz or spoke to her again. Through- out high school, Liz was quiet, mostly keeping to herself. She was a topnotch student and stayed out of trouble.

Liz had never taken up a close friendship with anyone for fear of being rejected like she had been with Sticks. It was clear Sticks wanted nothing to do with her, and so after high school she buried her head in college and decided she'd major in archaeology, paying special attention to Egyptology.

In college, Liz began to wonder about love. She was a radiant young beauty with sleek black hair and big greenish eyes that could seduce any young man, but she was too shy to pursue any of the men who approached her.

She argued in her history class about Egypt most often, but she hadn't dared to tell the story of her long forgotten roots. She knew no more than the stories Grandma Anta told her over the years.

Her history teacher wasn't convinced about Khemitology, calling it a conspiracy. Liz grew angry at the implications, 'til one day the teacher asked her to exit the classroom for being too argumentative and asked that she see him after class. The bell rang and the students exited the class room all looking Liz's way, but Liz didn't care.

Mr. Wellington, a well-known history teacher and in the learning establishment for over 20 years, spoke as Liz stood before him with her books in hand. "Liz, please sit down."

Liz took the first desk and sat quietly as she waited for the teacher to speak. He paced the room with his hands behind his back looking at the floor. "Liz, you are a wonderful, intelligent girl, heck! So intelligent that I wonder why you are at odds with the history of Egypt. Your arguments are invalid and there isn't information to support your claims. Why, Liz, tell me?" pleaded Mr. Wellington.

Liz replayed in her mind the stories of Grandma Anta. "Sir, I can assure you when I speak, It's from the heart. I believe wholly in Khemitology. I'm not shunting the art of archaeology, but I simply want to look at it from a different angle and answer the questions that aren't normally answered or known…"

Mr. Wellington interrupted, "I see, you are a seeker of truths. Well, this isn't really an answer, it's a calling. It isn't a philosophy or an activist class either. The class is about what's already been researched by our greatest predecessors. The facts Liz, are simply that. FACTS."

Liz stared at Mr. Wellington with a puzzled look. "Well don't just sit there, I know you wanna say something. What is it Liz?"

Liz stood up and finally answered, "Khemit is an old science, the mysticism of my ancestors. The way they once lived, the truth they held, a civilization beyond anyone's comprehension, even yours Mr. Wellington." Liz paused and Mr. Wellington smirked, as if he had been made fun of after 20 years of teaching Egyptology.

"I'm sorry, I don't follow. Every time you are asked to support the science, you withdraw. I've given you many chances to do so, why haven't you?" replied Mr. Wellington.

"I can't right now," said Liz. Grandma Anta's vision and storytelling entered her mind. "I can't!"

"That is not an answer either. I will no longer listen to your arguments. I will have to fail you," he said.

Liz yelled, "NO! Please, I can't fail. I'm doing the work regardless. I've handed in every project, my homework is always done, and you let me teach a class last week, please...."

Mr. Wellington stared at Liz and spoke again. "So why don't you tell me what's really going on?"

"My Grandma is Khemitian, as you know; that makes me half Khemitian. Mr. Wellington, she's been in a coma for five years now, and she started a story when I was eleven. Then she went to Egypt, and I've never heard the story again!"

She dashed out of the classroom, while Mr. Wellington ran after her. "Liz, stop, please come back," he shouted. But Liz kept running and jolted out of the building as fast as she could. She needed Grandma and she needed her now.

Liz awakened to the sounds of birds chirping outside that morning in May, the day after her little brawl with Mr. Wellington. She vowed to make things right with Mr. Wellington and even apologize for leaving so abruptly. But Liz was late that morning, and Mr. Wellington was waiting outside the classroom. "I am really sorry about your Grandma. I suppose this is hard on you, I owe you an apology."

"That's alright, no apology needed. I'm sorry for walking out, but I'll have you know that I will be an archeologist, and I will study Khemit. I will implement it in such a way where my voice will be heard, in honor of my ancestors!" replied the stubborn Liz.

Mr. Wellington couldn't help but smile and chuckle under his breath. He was left speechless by this ambitious teenager. He opened the door for Liz and welcomed her in class. She sat quietly and answered politely whenever Mr. Wellington called on her.

As Liz listened to Mr. Wellington drone on about accepted theories, she knew she would be someone great one day because of archaeology and Khemit. She wanted to follow in the footsteps of her great ancestor and predecessor Dr. Awyan, her long lost hero.

Soon it was June and the school year ended. Liz planned on taking some extra history classes over the summer. She scoured the internet one morning while sitting next to Grandma. Liz was deep in thought when she heard a voice, the deep voice of a young woman coming from outside Grandma's screen door. Liz approached the door cautiously.

"I rang the doorbell out front but no one answered. I figured you might be here," said the tall, lanky girl standing before Liz.

"I'm sorry, who are you?" asked Liz.

"It's Sticks, you fool!" replied Sticks laughing. Liz's eyes widened. The Sticks that stood before her was no longer a little girl. Her hair was blonde now, and her chest was beefed up in a tight bra. She was wearing tights and a tank top, so tight on her body, she looked as if she were right out of the local strip club.

Liz walked three steps back and said, "No, you're not the Sticks I once knew. Where have you been? You never called!"

"Oh. Liz, I'm sorry," Sticks said as she ran over and hugged Liz tightly. Liz didn't reciprocate so Sticks leaned back a step and stared at Liz. "I'm really sorry, so much has happened. I didn't mean to hurt you."

Liz thought of a time when the girls had been close, and those feelings quickly surfaced again. She put her anger aside. Sticks walked into Grandma's room, and Liz followed her. Sticks shed a tear and then spoke, "It's been five years; when she wakes it'll be like starting over. Not all beginnings are good, Liz." Sticks wiped her the tears from her eyes.

Liz held Sticks' hand to comfort her and led her to the kitchen table. Sticks sat while Liz made coffee for them. "How's life, Sticks?" asked Liz as she sat down. Her already knowing things were not well with Sticks.

"Where do I start? I mean, I was locked up in a group home the last four years. I was stuck there with kids my age. I did the best I could, and I had a baby last year Liz. They took him away, and he's in foster care now, awaiting adoption."

Liz 's eyes were filled with tears, and her heart ached for her friend.

"*Ahhhh* why am I telling you this? I'm a sorry excuse of a human being. I bet you're in college now and doing well, like you always said you would," said Sticks.

"I am. I'm taking archaeology and working on my degree. What about you?"

"Never mind me Liz. As you can tell, I turned out to be just like your Grandma said, a Hooligan. So, are you free this afternoon, want to hang out? I mean, I'm in the neighborhood for now," said Sticks.

"I'm sorry, but I have work to do. I'm looking to take more classes over the summer, and besides, you and I have drifted apart over the years. I don't know you anymore, Sticks. You can't just walk in here and pretend nothing ever happened." Liz stood up and picked up the coffee mugs and brought them over to the sink.

"Oh, for fuck's sake, Liz, really? You're gonna do this to me now? I thought we were cool? Did you ever stop in your tracks just once and think about me? My life? How tough I had to be to put things aside, walk the walk and talk the talk?" said Sticks.

Liz stood frozen in her tracks and then said, "I know it's been hard for you."

Sticks interrupted, "Hard! Hard she says! You don't know what it feels like to put on a happy face, while your grandfather repeatedly rapes you and beats you. I never once made you enter my world. I never told you everything, and now look. Some friend you are, little miss "know it all" with the perfect family and the perfect grades. I wish you well, I'm outta here. FUCK THIS SHIT!" Sticks grabbed her purse and walked out the door.

Liz ran after her yelling, "Wait, I'm sorry Sticks. I had no clue!" But it was too late. Sticks got in her car and drove off, leaving fresh tire marks on the asphalt. Liz stood motionless with her hands crossed over her chest. She watched Sticks drive away and now felt horrible for letting her go. The years had passed and Sticks had stayed away for the good of their friendship. She hadn't been selfish at all.

That night Liz spoke to God about a little child who was molested and physically beaten every other day. Liz couldn't stop it, and her heart was in pieces. Sticks turned out to be a messed up young woman with no future. Liz replayed all the images in her mind back to a time, not so long ago, when Sticks awoke from her coma telling Liz, "You don't need to see that." She concealed it all from Liz, and Liz was slowly putting the pieces of the puzzle together. Sticks was right after all. She may have been messed up, but one thing was sure, Sticks did love Liz as a sister.

Grandma Anta's caregiver could be heard yelling from the back yard, so Liz ran to the back of the house. Liz's heart raced even faster now as the caregiver yelled, "She's awake, she's awake!" Liz had the biggest grin on her face, and the caregiver kept yelling to call the doctor. Grandma Anta was back!

She finally spoke and stared at Liz for a long time.

Liz held her hands. "Who are you?" said Anta and Liz laughed.

"Grandma! It's me Lizzy!" Anta stared at Liz knowing it had been a long time and began to sob uncontrollably. "No Grandma, please don't cry, you're okay. Look at you, you haven't even aged!"

"Look at you now, oh my! You are a beauty, a spitting image of Nefertiti herself," said Anta.

Liz laughed and said, "People have told me this often, but I don't think so. C'mon, Grandma don't be silly,"

Liz's eyes filled with tears and joy the rest of the day while the doctor attended to Anta. Tests were being done to ensure Grandma Anta was stabilized. She was under 24-hour watch. Stick's visit that day may have triggered something in Grandma, Liz thought. Maybe it was nature's way of wanting to defend the young from danger. Whatever it was, Liz thought it was the saddest day, as well as the best day all rolled up in one.

Grandma wanted badly to get out of bed and complained about her buttocks. She was feisty at times, but she was a temple of knowledge.

The family was told Grandma might need extra help for walking, so Justin bought a walker for Grandma to use until she could replace it with her cane. Grandma passed a cat scan and other related tests which meant that for the time being Grandma was in good shape.

Sticks had come and gone from Liz's mind over the last few days. Grandma entered the hospital for more tests, and on the day of her dismissal, a party was thrown for Grandma Anta at the Hawann residence for the entire neighborhood.

It just never felt right without Sticks. Where was Sticks? What was she doing? Liz watched the stars closely and prayed for Sticks. She prayed that God may watch over her and keep her safe. It was all she could do for Sticks now. Liz watched the beautiful lit up sky when she heard Grandma's walker hit the door frame.

"Wait, Grandma, I'll help you with that," Liz said.

"Nonsense, I got this." Anta struggled, but she finally entered the room.

"You have grown, and I missed it all. You look wonderful, Lizzy. Anta sat on one of Liz's new chairs upholstered in silver.

"Grandma, it's late; you should be sleeping," said Liz who now took a seat on her bed and looked Grandma's way.

"Please! I've been sleeping for five years! And besides, I may have been Sleeping Beauty, but I haven't lost my memory, and if it serves me correctly, you and I have an appointment!" said Anta as she winked Liz's way and blew her a kiss.

Liz was smitten by Grandma and her beautiful ways. She loved her to death. "Grandma, you just came out of the hospital, I think you should rest."

"No, you have waited too long, and guess what! We don't have to wait for bedtime anymore. You're all grown up now and this means I can tell the story the way it was intended to be told," replied Anta.

"What do you mean?" asked Liz.

"Well, when you were younger, I had to leave out some parts, but you're almost 18 now."

Liz laughed. "*Ohhhh*, I see, sex and profanity!"

Anta smiled, slyly.

"If it's any consolation, Grandma, we learned about sex in the fifth grade. I'm no stranger to its stories. I know in those days, they were very sexually promiscuous," replied Liz.

"Yes, well, I hope that is a stranger to you. Wait for marriage, please," insisted Grandma.

Liz blushed at her words and her open-minded thoughts. Liz wasn't attracted to marriage or having children. She thought of those things as being thousands of miles away.

"Well," said Anta, "at any rate, the Pharaoh was a tower of sex. She invited men and woman to her bed, at any time. Khafa was worried because now the land was being neglected. Prosperity was running dry like a well. Gossip about the temple spread as rapidly as forest fires. The council had not been in favor of Pharaoh Aketu`s behavior. Khafa was slowly being nudged in a direction where she would have to change things, and change them fast for the sake of the Pharaoh and the land.

Now entering Aketu`s chambers, where she lay on her bed with a man beside her, Khafa made no apology. Instead, she cleared her throat and coughed a little to let them know she was there and stood straight facing the couple with her hands behind her back.

"Khafa, you enter without notice. May I ask what is so important that it couldn't wait?" asked the Pharaoh as she caressed the face of the young man beside her. She hadn't been angry but rather surprised.

"My Pharaoh, we need to have words, alone," replied Khafa, who by now was signaling for the boy to leave the chambers. The boy was younger than the Pharaoh. He was buff and beautiful, and very well endowed. Aketu was sad to let him go. She had exquisite taste in men, and she only chose the gorgeous and the well-endowed. She never had an ugly lover, male or female.

"My Pharaoh, please, this is very important. The city is starving, and it's been six months of famine again. The droughts haven't helped, and your recreational activities have the whole Kingdom gossiping. Your image is that of an uncaring, selfish whore," said Khafa with no hesitation.

The Pharaoh turned immediately towards Khafa and looked her in the eye. "No one calls me a whore!" As she spoke those words, she lifted her hand to slap Khafa, but Khafa was wise. She knew the Pharaoh would react this way, so she stopped her hand in mid-air.

"No, you listen to me and you listen well. If I am to be your appointed guide and right hand, you must live up to your title before it is taken away from you. The right hand is to be obeyed at all times, and you have not the experience of ruling a Kingdom. You must stop your ways now!" Khafa slowly put down her hand and both stared into each other's eyes deeply, Aketu had no choice but to bow down and be submissive to Khafa's words.

"Very well, I see you are strong willed and determined. We shall follow this path. What is our next move?" asked the Pharaoh, hating every minute of the submissive game.

"We will begin with a council meeting, but first we must face the facts about your behavior. Then we move on to business. We meet in the council chamber shortly," said Khafa with conviction. "Now get dressed."

"It is late; can't this wait?" asked Aketu.

"No, the business of your population must never wait; they've been waiting too long!" said Khafa, as she ordered the chamber maid to fetch the Pharaoh's clothes.

"Won't you dress me?" asked Aketu.

"No, the maidens will see to this from now on; it is not my job anymore,' said Khafa as she exited the chambers.

Arriving at the council chambers 20 minutes later, the Pharaoh sat down and everyone was seated. Aketu knew she was at the mercy of her right hand, Khafa, who was wise and intelligent, so she let her have center stage and act as her advocate before the 22 members.

"It is with great apology we stand before you today. The ways of the Pharaoh will be corrected immediately." Khafa was interrupted by yelling and raised voices. Aketu grew worried and Khafa whispered in her ear. "Sit quietly and let me handle the crowd." As she spoke to Aketu, the crowd grew angrier and demanded explanations.

"Enough!" yelled Khafa. The council stopped in fright and so did the Pharaoh. "Now, it has come to our attention that this behavior is deeply frowned upon and with good reason. We, the staff of the Pharaoh, will guarantee the safety of the land and bring back prosperity for all with new and upcoming projects."

Khafa was interrupted again as one man stood up and spoke. "And how can we trust the words of the right hand? You knew about the Pharaoh's behavior. Why haven't you stopped it prior? This new dynasty brings destruction to Egypt. Not an heir has been produced yet from a royal wedding, and who will have her now? Her impurity brings shame on the land."

Another councilman stood up and agreed. "Indeed, not even the dogs will have her now!" The room stood silent, and Aketu bowed her head in shame and looked on Khafa to save the day.

"You will not call your Pharaoh a whore, you have one warning before all. Never, and I repeat, never use those words again in this palace or any other part of this realm. For If I hear any of you plotting against her, I will have you killed myself!"

Khafa now spoke of business matters. "The announcement of the new projects will be spoken in public before the land, and this will reassure the population that they have not been forgotten. These projects will take time, much coin and wealth to bring forth for all."

Another man rose from his seat and spoke out, "Safety from droughts is our first concern above all others. We cannot wait on this, my priestess!"

Khafa countered, "Yes, this is truth, but what have you done for your drought victims and the safety of this land from this disastrous event? Are you not the man who controls your district? Are you not to see your workers putting this into practice? Do you have a blue print of your inventions or ideas?"

"If I haven't the go ahead or coin to see this project through, then I cannot move forward," replied the foolish man. Khafa raised an eyebrow, and Aketu tried to speak, but Khafa silenced her.

Khafa proceeded with her speech and added that the Pharaoh would wed in the short weeks to follow. They would seek a prince from the Doggone culture, as there was no one available in Egypt. Aketu was the last of her Dynasty, and not even cousins were available to wed. This seemed to sit well with the council, but they were still worried about the drought.

Khafa slowly paced the room behind the throne of the Pharaoh, thinking of ways to address them. She wondered how they would react to the next announcement.

Chapter 5

"OMNIPOTENT POWER"

Grandma paused and took a drink of water. "Okay, now for the exciting party. Are you still with me, Liz?"

Liz sat up straighter in her bed and said, "I'm ready, Grandma."

Grandma continued with the story. So, finally, Aketu said suddenly to the council, "I am calling a short recess so the priestess and I can have words alone." The council left the chambers in a hurry because they were afraid of displeasing the two women.

As soon as they left, the Pharaoh spoke to Khafa in confidence. "I will marry, but I will always have my way in private. I don't even mind if my new husband allows it. He may also do as he pleases."

Khafa grabbed the Pharaoh's hands and said, "You will allow yourself to be Queen, and give the title of Pharaoh to your new husband. Do as you please in this regard and keep it hidden and secret. Go far if you must, but you will be Queen and this is your objective and the path to straightening out your reputation." Aketu then spoke, 'What is this other project you have in mind?'

"*Ahhh* yes, the project. I will announce this before all; this is something so grand, you will never believe it yourself, my Pharaoh."

Aketu smiled and left this idea in capable hands.

"It will save you and you will be loved for it, remembered and praised for it in centuries to come. Not even your husband-to-be will have the glory; you'll have it all for yourself," said Khafa.

Aketu loved this idea, and now asked the guards to bring the council back in the chamber,

"Be seated," said Khafa as the men entered the room.

"Allow me to show you modern Egypt!" Khafa un-scrolled several papyruses and spread them out before the council members. Their jaws opened as they looked on the documents before them.

Khafa

Aketu whispered in Khafa's ear, "Care to explain?"

Khafa spoke to Aketu, "This is the future of Egypt, depicted for your eyes only. Well, for the moment that is. These are no ordinary monuments as our great Kufu, King of Egypt, produced them. We will recreate these for one purpose only, the purpose of light by night!"

The men began to ask questions so Khafa explained the principle of "light by night" to them.

"Apologies my priestess," the men said after her explanation. "But how have you come across this, and what is it you are trying to achieve, this 'light by night' you speak of?"

"I have come across this through my studies of the people in my culture, the science and spirituality that only Khemit brings," replied Khafa.

Aketu raised an eyebrow and was confused by her words. Then another man spoke out. "This is unheard of and preposterous! Are you saying you want to have daylight in night? It is impossible!"

"Is it?" asked Khafa. "The plans are laid out before you. Do you not believe this was researched and experimented prior to this announcement?"

Khafa was interrupted by yet the same member but silenced him quickly. "Allow me," said Khafa as yet again another guard came to the table with a strange concoction. It was an oval shaped glass jar that produced light! When Khafa displayed her project and its functions using water to get the light to shine, it worked!

The council was in awe. The same man that stood up before stood up again and yelled, "This is sorcery, black magic; it is no wonder it comes from a priestess. Your trade before all others. You seek war and destruction; such things are forbidden. You seek to disrupt and bring chaos upon us; I will not be a part of such." The man slammed down his hands on the table.

Khafa commanded, "If you will not join us, then you are against us. Kill him!" The members of the council stayed quiet as the guards grabbed the man from behind. He pleaded to be spared, and the Pharaoh mercilessly denied him.

The man exited the room kicking and screaming while being dragged away. "You are doomed. You hear me, doomed I say!" The rest of the council hadn't even looked Khafa's way for fear of being next.

"Anyone else care to join your friend?" asked Khafa. No one answered but eyes and heavy sighs were coming from the doubters. Khafa caught on, but didn't say a word. She proceeded with questions, answering them all one by one. The conclusion was that pyramids would be built for light, having electricity all through the land powered by water underneath the pyramids! Construction was to commence before the future King was to arrive, right on the Giza strip and along the Nile for easy accessibility."

Liz stopped Grandma Anta's story. "I knew it Grandma! This proves the Tesla theory all too well. He's the only one who got it right!"

Grandma Anta said, "Yes, the only one, and yet, it was still considered a theory. The world couldn't be further from the mark!"

Liz sat in despair. How would she ever put this into practice, a practice she wanted to be a part of? Now she felt more alone in these teachings than ever. "Go on. Grandma," said Liz.

"Okay, dear," said Grandma. "I'll continue. So…where was I? Oh yes, the meeting. Well, the meeting went on for hours. Aketu saw the sunrise coming up, and Khafa was well into the second phase of the construction. It was a monstrous task, one that would take approximately 20 years to complete. By this time Aketu would be well in her forties. They had all agreed that this would shape the future of Egypt and that it would bring forth new technology and life. Some of the members who hadn't been so receptive at first eventually accepted the project and its value to Egypt.

When the meeting was adjourned, Khafa called on her guards and whispered, "Kill anyone who opposes this plan."

Khafa

"No!, Have you lost your mind? We'll have no one sitting in for them," said Aketu.

"The first rule of reign is to remove those who will betray you, even if it means the ones who reign beside you. Doubters have no place here," said Khafa. "I'm going to bed now. It's been a long day."

Khafa had never answered one question, the question of how she really got those blue-prints. The truth was in her earlier years when she married the priest Hackatu in her own culture. He had produced these ideas with his team of scholars in Khemit. Khafa murdered her husband in his sleep after word came they were to make their way to Luxor and work for the dynasty there as their priests. Khafa knew one day she could talk anyone in power into making this a reality. She had the skill and ability with her charm and beauty, and she even used her body from time to time to get all she desired. She climbed her way to the top by using her wits and made it very far, as far as the right hand now.

It was clear that Khafa was searching for power by any means possible; her interests lay only there. She played on the weakness of the Pharaoh like she was a marionette, but she would also bring good to the future Queen. Khafa loved the game of playing on the sidelines without having all of the attention focused on her.

The Pharaoh was intoxicated by Khafa's display of power, and later that morning Aketu approached her and kissed her on the lips, coaxing her to sex. Khafa refused and instead suggested a new maiden in her place.

Aketu was juvenile and this offended her a little, but Khafa persuaded her that pleasure and business did not do well together.

After her rejection by Khafa, Aketu drank away the hours and had sex with anyone available. The Pharaoh stayed drunk for days, until she awoke to find Khafa staring at her. "I hope you had enough. You will bathe now, and you will wash away all your sins in the Nile. You'll appear before your people tonight when the sun is down and the air is cooler. This will make for a better speech," said Khafa, as she helped the

Pharaoh up to a boat waiting to take her to a secluded bathing spot made for her.

"What about my king? When shall he come?" asked Aketu.

"I leave tomorrow. I will go and plead for his hand, and I will make it so appealing he will have no other choice," said Khafa.

Aketu laughed and Khafa joined in. Aketu was genuine and naïve, Khafa played on this very well. She loved the Pharaoh as her own, but the order of business was a priority she would never reveal to her. They needed a strong Queen and Khafa was the only heartless beast to mold her into this figure and image. There was no one better for the task at hand. A great queen Egypt would get.

Riding out the day after, Khafa was accompanied by Egypt's army and some councilmen who had become very close to Khafa--some she would trust with her life.

Well into the core of Western Africa lay the Doggone culture, a civilization much like the Egyptians, Khafa felt right at home here, since she spoke the language. She asked to be seen by their King and Queen when she entered the village. The people had been very accepting of her presence. Arriving at the King's temple was an easy journey.

Khafa knew the King and Queen had children and their eldest, Takenrunh was their 19-year-old Prince. She had heard rumors that he was handsome beyond belief, strong and built well for love making and reproducing. He earned all his merits in battles, hunting and gaming activities throughout the Kingdom.

At the temple, Khafa was greeted with the utmost respect. A five-day itinerary was in place to display all of the Prince's talents and abilities. When Takenrunh met with Khafa for the first time that evening in a ceremony of welcoming, he was mesmerized by her beauty. Khafa couldn't contain her feelings either as she approached the Prince and bowed before him. She handed him a gift from the Pharaoh. The gift box contained Egyptian jewelry for men, specifically gold rings and wrist bracelets fit for a future King.

Khafa

"Allow me, my Prince. These are for you. Our Pharaoh sends her very best," said Khafa as her heart raced quickly and her ankles shook like she had been drunk on wine. The Prince extended his hands and held hers while taking the box.

"Indeed, she does send her very best," said the Prince, eyeing Khafa. Whatever Khafa did was through praying and her rituals, but this was not something she planned or prayed about. She thought she would have to persuade the young Prince to his destiny by using sex and forcing herself on him.

Now that her plan was in place, she desired the young prince immensely. Later that night when food and delicious wines were being served, she teased him and played hard to get. When the music came on she and her priestesses were asked to perform their ritual dance. Khafa took center stage again while eight of her priestesses stood behind her. They danced all in sync, not missing a beat.

The Prince was in a trance, and she seduced him to her every move. She was tempting and alluring. Her eyes danced around him and invited him to her body. Her breasts were bountiful and her nipples were hard beneath her translucent dress. It was clear the Prince wanted every inch of her that night, and she purposely orchestrated her talents for she had to have him first.

The Prince was no stranger to sex. It was also believed he had fathered children already and was quite the sexual beast roaming the realm. The King and Queen noticed how much in lust the Prince and the priestess were, and they seemed delighted by this turn of events. But the men from the council weren't very happy about the display.

The Prince was not a lover of wines; he loved women instead, and Khafa hadn't felt this way in a long time. The music was over and all applauded. The Prince was now hungry with desire for Khafa.

The rest of the celebration was in full swing, but Khafa made her way outside, coaxing the young Prince to follow her. Khafa waited patiently with a goblet of wine watching the moonlit sky. The Prince followed and stood behind her. She could feel the warmth of his breath on her neck.

"Do all the women in Egypt dance like this?" asked the shy, young Prince.

"Are all princes manly like you but display shyness?" asked Khafa who turned to face the handsome prince. The Prince laughed and spoke.

"Forgive me, I'm not usually shy, a woman like you, is so intimidating, I'm...."

Khafa interrupted and pulled herself close to him. The five-foot Khafa looked up to six-foot Prince. "I'm what, scary?" She gazed upon his muscular chest and caressed it very lightly with her fingernails. The Prince shut his eyes and sighed with pleasure. His manhood began to grow. Khafa could feel him against her body. She laughed and the Prince opened his eyes to meet her devilish green ones. She could see that he was hot with desire for her, but she did not want to appear too easily won.

Pulling away, she said, "Forgive me, it's late. I must retire to my chambers, because we have a long day tomorrow." He grabbed her from behind and whispered in her ear. "I've never met a woman like you. Everyone throws themselves at me, and here you are, resisting!"

"Good night, my Prince!" she said and then walked away. Khafa knew she'd have him sooner rather than later, and this brought a smile to her face. Entering her chambers that night, she removed her clothing in the dark. As she did so she saw a shadow move across the room. She screamed in fright, but a torch drew near and the shadow was revealed to her. It was the King! The King, too, was infatuated with her and tried to force himself upon her.

"King Ranteh, I cannot," she said, but the King grabbed her forcefully by her wrists. She screamed and fought, remembering a time where she was often forced to have sex with many powerful men and pretending to enjoy it.

Khafa

"If you want to take my son to reign in Egypt, you'll do exactly what you are told. Now come, I am ready. You will sit on me and ride me like a horse." Khafa did exactly what she was told, tears falling down her face as she mounted the King. He sucked on her breasts moaning in pleasure. The King was well-endowed. Khafa hadn't any sexual relations with anyone in months. She began to like the experience and let loose her sexual powers.

"I knew you'd like it, you dirty little whore," the King said spitefully. But, the Prince heard moans when passing by this chamber and stopped to listen. He opened the door slightly and quietly and saw his father and Khafa naked together in bed.

Khafa was embarrassed and the King ran out of the chambers. The Prince ran after him threatening to tell the Queen. Khafa was left alone and wondered if this journey was worth it. She came for the love of the Pharaoh and nothing more.

Morning came quickly and games and tournaments were to be had, but the King had left on business with his knights to another land and would not be returning for months. So Khafa thought she caught a lucky break since she wouldn't be bothered by his demands anymore. A bigger issue was at hand now, and that was one not to be taken lightly.

Khafa had to persuade a jealous Prince to be the ruler of Egypt. She approached the Prince before his games and apologized. "I'm sorry, but he forced me," said Khafa.

The prince looked at her with disgust. "Why would I come to Egypt and rule, when I can rule here one day and have all the commodities laid out before me? All the women I want and enough riches to live on til the afterlife?" said the Prince reached for his gear.

Khafa gently helped him with his armor. "Please, don't touch me," said the Prince. Khafa backed away and rolled her eyes.

The Prince participated in the games, fighting angrily and brutally.

Khafa headed back to the temple instead of watching the rest of the tournament, and thought to herself she only had four days left to win over the Prince. She thought about making him jealous with another man, but that would only add more fuel to the fire and anger him further. She thought about a love incantation, but it was already too late, He was in love with her already. Khafa was out of options for the first time in her life, and this was a horrible thing.

Evening drew near and Khafa remembered the past night and how she had seduced the Prince. But, she realized, it was more than seduction, they were truly "in love." She worried this would bring utter destruction to them both if the Pharaoh found out. Aketu wasn't the jealous type, and she had declared her love of entertainment versus the love of her King, so maybe Khafa would be spared. It was eating up her mind as she sat alone wondering if the Prince was flirting with other women. She wondered if he cared for her at all.

Suddenly the Prince appeared in her chambers. "You have no right to feel like this," he said as he grabbed her by her arms.

She yelled back, "You have no right to do what you did."

He let her go, backed off and gazed upon her lovingly. "You love me!" he said softly. She turned and looked the other way and didn't breathe or speak a word. He turned her around to meet his face. "Say it!" he yelled.

"Never!" she cried. At that moment he kissed her, and she kissed back fiercely. They clung to each other tightly, kissing each other heavily and passionately. He kissed her neck as he slowly removed her clothes. When he entered her, she moaned so loudly it triggered the beast in him. She begged for more as he aggressively entered her time after time. Scratching his back with her razor sharp nails, the Prince groaned in pain and pleasure. She mounted him skillfully and wound her legs tightly around him. He cried out in pleasure as he totally lost control of his body and senses. Afterwards, he gently fondled her breasts, the breasts he longed for a day earlier.

The love making hadn't lasted more than 20 minutes, but both had enjoyed each other tremendously. Neither the Prince nor Khafa ever knew love like this in their lives. They lay in each other's arms for a long time, and then Khafa spoke. "I don't know what you've done to me, but we are in deep trouble."

The Prince smiled. "It must be love; I have never felt strongly for any other woman. You are magical and sexy. How can any man ignore you?" He placed his head on her stomach and caressed her soft hips.

"You must go before we are caught," she said sadly.

"Caught from whom? We do not care about promiscuity here. We are free to do as we please," said the Prince who ran his tongue up her body to her breasts.

They kissed gently and arousal resurfaced once more. The Prince stood up and lifted her and placed her feet on the ground while they were still locked in a kiss. She got out of his grip and pinned him to the temple wall. She slid down his body and took him in her mouth. The high priestess was a phenomenal lover. The Prince felt the most pleasure he had ever had that night. He knew this would not be his last time with the high priestess.

Chapter 6

"Tower of Knowledge"

Arriving in Luxor weeks later, the Queen, former   Pharaoh was still practicing her old ways. She looked a wreck and she was inhospitable when the celebration ceremonies began. The Prince offered her Doggone jewelry and sat next to her as she demanded. "I have no interest in a real husband," said the Queen. "I saw what my father did to my mother for many years. There was no love or respect between them. You and I will copulate in the interest of producing heirs, but I have no hold on you, nor shall you have any hold me. As Pharaoh for the time being, I command you now and always to keep this oath." Aketu smiled at the men around her in a flirtatious way.

The Prince was relieved for this meant he could be with Khafa, which was the real reason why he had come to Egypt. The Prince swore he would uphold his oath, but there were rules attached to these stipulations. They would always have to uphold a loving way in public and in front of their future children. "Agreed, my Pharaoh. I will be true to this, for I myself seek the company of many, or perhaps one love," he foolishly replied.

Aketu stared at him with evil eyes and spoke again. "No, it is forbidden to love another; you may be with whom you choose, but not love. It will shame the dynasty and tarnish our name."

"Very well, as you wish," said the Prince as he bowed before the Pharaoh. He then made an exit from the grand room.

Prince Takenrunh now grew worried, for the love he felt for Khafa had to be concealed. Takenrunh was already 20 and Khafa wasn't getting any younger either. She was 5 years older than him. She would have to quickly orchestrate everything, including all the plots and secret plans to meet up for lovemaking. Khafa couldn't stop her desires and neither could Takenrunh.

Khafa

Construction for the pyramids had begun, and men by the thousands worked night and day. They were well fed, eating fish and nuts, mangoes and other exotic fruits, drinking wines and mead to keep them strong and healthy for this 20-year project. On their journey to Egypt, Khafa explained her scientific and spiritual approach toward her project.

The Doggone culture had never shunted the Khemit's ways, but rather embraced them as well. The Prince was floored when he saw the sites being excavated and the foundations built. It was structured so that the water of the Nile would flood the aquifers of the pyramid foundations. He had sworn to Khafa that he would come and supervise the sites and work if he had to once he was Pharaoh. He would do anything to get away from the terrible Queen.

Khafa understood the Queen better than most. She knew what it was like to lose one's parents at an early age. She, too, had been a victim of raiders who killed off her entire tribe except for her and a few others who had managed to hide underground. Khafa's mother and father was brutally killed trying to defend all they had. Khafa was sympathetic, so she let the Pharaoh alone. After all she needed to feel like she still had some powers left to reign and make her own decisions.

***

The royal wedding was grand and the Prince was now crowned Egypt's new Pharoah, Takenrunh the First. The marriage had to be consumated at once, and so after a short ceremony, the new Pharoah and Queen lay beside each other, not fancying one another in the slightest. The Queen decided she would have a few goblets of wine to ease the tension between them, and the Pharoah did the same. Before too long the Pharoah entered the Queen. The Pharoah wasn't happy and with every thrust, he thought of Khafa, it was torturous and long, and the Queen felt nothing for the him either, not even a little pleasure. But the Pharoah's thrusts intensified as the image of Khafa came to his mind. They both finally reached their sexual heights, and the Pharoah released his seed inside of the Queen. They were hoping she would get pregnant soon, so they would eventually stop pretending in private. They were utterly disgusted by each other, but they had enough respect to keep their relationship amicable.

Six months later there was still no sign of a baby. Khafa and the Pharoah met every other night to have passionate sex. Sometimes they satisfied themselves by ditches near the Nile, and sometimes in secret hiding places in forests and boats. The excitement and adrenaline rush they got from this was intoxicating.

Then on the seventh month of her marriage, the Queen fell ill one morning and her monthly didn't come. It was a sure sign now that a baby was on the way. The council had been ecstatic about the news, and the Kingdom started to finally put their resentment of the Queen aside. When the Queen announced the news to the Pharoah, she addressed him as "my King," and he became known as King of Egypt henceforth."

"Wow, Grandma! You are so descriptive. You hold nothing back!" said Liz whose cheeks had reddened.

"No need to blush. I'm telling you how things really happened."

Liz smiled and spoke again. "I know of Khafa's plans, Grandma. The energy is still palpable in these sites today, I've done my research, and I've majored in Nikola Tesla's free energy projects class. His Long Island tower was almost the spitting image of what the Egyptians had already built thousands of years before."

Grandma exclaimed, "Yes! Indeed, so you believe in the Khemit and the people of the band of peace, my people!"

"I do, but much more than this; there's a staggering amount of proof all over Egypt that machine tooling was used. Chisel's alone could never have perfected the temples, statues and all they built. So, if machine tooling was used, this means that energy collected made electricity and electricity powered the tools, thus bringing us this evidence!" said Liz who was master in the mystic teachings.

Khafa

"You've grown so much, Lizzy dear. In five years you have become a pillar of knowledge, a beautiful girl and a gorgeous soul. I love you Lizzy!" said Grandma as she reached and hugged her tightly.

"It's good to have you back, Grandma," replied Lizzy. Grandma wasn't providing Lizzy with the science of Khemit. She was providing her with something much more than science or history. She told a story passed down to her from her ancestors, a story they strongly believed in because it had never changed throughout its existence.

In Khemit it is believed that the rise and fall of the Nile, along with its droughts, storms and heavy rains, would generate enough energy throughout the pyramid to illuminate its surroundings and create light by night. Liz speculated that on the American dollar the secret code is well hidden to most but very much exposed to the individuals who are aware; the pyramid depicted the Illuminati and its existence all too well. A bigger connection was at play here. Illuminati hid the secrets, or cracked the code at some point in time, and this subliminal message was left on a back burner for all eyes who ever gazed upon an American dollar bill. Liz also learned by her own research and not those taught in any class, that tour guides today are never to point out certain images that were depicted on temple walls.

Were scientists and archeologists or Egyptian authorities restricting the common folk from learning the truth in the name of protecting science? Theories, conspiracies and hard evidence were scattered all around Egypt, and some of the most renowned physicists, biological engineers and astrologists had no other choice but to conclude that Dr. Awyan's findings about the mysticism of Khmeit was very much close to the actual events, if not the truth in itself.

Liz remembered her research very well, and knew there was also evidence that pointed to a higher knowledge of technology by the ancient Egyptians, like our helicopters and airplanes of today. Many such drawings appeared on their temple walls. How did they know about such advanced modes of transportation? Had they built any? A reasonable explanation was argued about these images by archeologists and scientists as well. Over time, some of these images have been destroyed or chiseled over. This seemed more than a coincidence to Liz.

She wanted passionately to unfold Egypt's greatest conspiracies and cover ups. Modern mankind, in Liz's opinion, was nowhere near as advanced as the Khemitians. So she began a journey of truth. She opened social media sites and posted things like, "Illuminati is the devil," in order to draw attention to herself. She hoped to have a constant flood of people commenting on her threads. That was exhausting and archaeology was starting to take a back seat.

She often spoke to herself. "Ok, I just requested 20 friendships today; the more on my page the merrier. C'mon Liz, let's do this thang!" Liz was obsessed. Then when Mr. Wellington failed her in one assignment, Liz began to cry. She knew she had to shift back and drop the page for a while. It was becoming an unbearably huge task. She was constantly hounded for her actions on social media, blocked from different procedures, and pictures were taken down by the internal police force. There were messages sent to her about violating the code of conduct, and 20,000 of her members disappeared over night. She was cut off completely, and it only proved to be a blessing in time.

At school students hounded her about starting up her page again, but the threats she received from the CIA and other secret organizations took their toll on her. She was done with the Internet, at least for the time being. Things became even tougher for Liz. Even though her teachers hadn't dared to approach her or her beliefs, they were anything but friendly. They just stared her down or looked the other way. She was hated and loved, and yet, she didn't care all that much. She often thought of rallying this ideology, but when Mr. Wellington advised her it wouldn't be wise for her career, Liz took three steps back, retreated to her cave of archaeology and never looked back.

She refused to hear any more of Grandma's story or teachings. Instead, Liz threw herself into her studies and passed every project, assignment and quiz. Her 18th birthday had come and gone now, and some of her classmates celebrated an outing with her on that particular night, but they were nothing like having Sticks around.

Sticks had been the center of her universe once, and it was hard to forget her. She tried looking for her on social media on a number of occasions, but to no avail. Google hadn't provided her with any more information either. It was as if she had dropped off the face of the planet. Some of the worst thoughts crossed her mind. "Is she dead? Lord, please give me a sign!" she whispered to herself often, but a sign never came.

Liz's parents, Catherine and Justin, took a long awaited vacation to Europe that year, leaving Grandma Anta and Liz behind. Grandma was fully recovered and raring to go back to Egypt. Although Liz had gained much popularity with her school mates, she had now begun having thoughts of having a boyfriend. She wanted someone to hug and kiss and perhaps venture into the sea of love or at least experience it for the first time. Becoming a woman was hard for Liz. She had only ever done one thing for herself, and that was to immerse herself in her education.

She wondered if a man would understand all she held dear, or if he would be the thorn in her side. It was conflicting, and as time went on, a new school year started. Back in Mr. Wellington's class, she often heard him yelling, "Elizabeth, please have seat," She liked to help other students who were having trouble understanding concepts, so she often ignored Mr. Wellington. A little rebel had emerged, and she carried the torch of conspiracy on her back. Some days she longed for more experience, an experience that could slowly kill her future.

One day in class as Liz was lost in the conspiracy cloud, the door swung open and a young man stood before her. "I'm sorry, is this Mr. Wellington's class?" he asked nervously. He adjusted his glasses and shifted the books in his hands.

"It is, and you are 20 minutes late. Do you have a note explaining your tardiness?" replied Mr. Wellington. Liz stared at the young man with infatuation. The young man handed the note to Mr. Wellington who read its contents.

At that moment the young man made eye contact with Liz and froze completely where he stood. Mr. Wellington spoke again, but the young man was still in a trance. They were both floating on a cloud 'til Mr. Wellington interrupted with his usual yelling.

"Mr. Rick Cotts, are you in the class or in another world? Please have a seat!" Rick ran to find a place while the whole class laughed at the display of attraction between them both. Later Liz would find out that Rick Cotts had just moved in the neighborhood. He transferred from another college, and he was quite the bookworm. He also was a loner and kept mostly to himself. Liz thought he was devastatingly handsome underneath his glasses. His grey blue eyes were shaped like almonds, and his sleek black hair, was straight and long. He was tall and lanky with loose clothing hiding a well-built body.

He was a starter for the college's football team and proved to be an exceptional athlete, but, most of all, he was an archaeology genius in class, probably the next Howard Carter, she thought. Months went on, and she kept a close eye on him without being too noticeable.

Liz later learned that Rick kept a close eye on her, too. He often looked at her social media pages, but couldn't muster up the courage to ask for her friendship. He would often pause and speak to himself. "Nefertiti in the flesh, how will she ever date me? I'm not good enough!" he repeatedly said.

During those same months, Liz spoke to herself as well. "*Ughhhh*, so handsome, so little time. If he really liked me, he would have asked me out by now." One night Liz sat at the dinner table playing with her food and making lines in her mashed potatoes. Grandma, who had been watching her for a while, asked, "Lizzy, you are not eating, why?"

"I'm not all that hungry," replied Liz, who was also staring into outer space.

"Lizzy, first the conspiracy incident and now this? I know when something is not right, tell me!" demanded Grandma Anta.

"Ohhh okayyy!" replied Liz. "I like this guy at school, but I don't think he likes me back."

Grandma Anta smiled and took a chair beside Liz and softly asked, "How do you know, he doesn't?"

"Well, every time I look at him or try to make eye contact like the first day we met, he pretends to look away. It's been four months Grandma. He should have asked me out by now!" exclaimed Liz.

"That is nonsense, Lizzy. Have you ever thought maybe he's very shy, or maybe feels inadequate? There are such feelings you know!" said Anta. Liz shrugged her shoulders and tossed her head to the side and nodded in approval. "If you don't give it a try, you'll never know!" said Anta.

"Oh no! Let's not go there, Grandma. I will not make the first move. I believe it's for the man to do," said Liz as she got up from the table and took her plate to the sink. She threw her whole meal down the sink disposalint and headed for her room.

As Liz climbed the stairs, she could hear Grandma Anta mumble, "Stubborn! Just like her father and grandfather!"

***

January arrived and still not a look or conversation had taken place between Rick and Liz. Liz begun to lose interest all together. There were other girls who had thrown themselves at Rick, some very appealing, but Rick hadn't paid any attention to them. Liz started to question whether he was gay and interested in boys until one cold February morning.

That morning Liz slipped on a banana peel on the front stairs of the college. Rick had been nearby and came to her rescue. "Elizabeth? You all right?" asked Rick as he extended a hand. She gladly took it, and when she bounced up her eyes met his. He was so devilishly handsome; she couldn't help but smile. Her shy side surfaced as she bowed her head.

"I'm fine now, thank you." She couldn't help but add the "now." It came naturally.

Rick smiled back and then said, "Wait, let me get the door for you. I see you're limping a little. You sure you'll be fine?" asked Rick.

Liz tried walking a little more, but her leg was in pain and she screeched a little, "Ouch!"

"Okay, I think I'll take you to the nurse's station. Here, hang on to me," commanded Rick who was more than happy to come to her aid.

They sat outside the nurse's office most of the morning. It was a busy day for the nurse, so Rick thought he'd break the ice. "So...come here often?"

Liz laughed hysterically at the comment. Rick joined in the laughing fit as well. It was obvious they had deep feelings for each other, and this incident was a blessing. Rick leaned over and kissed her gently and tenderly on the lips. Liz let it happen and was on a cloud and then class was over. They looked at each other once more in total lust for one another. Rick stood up gathered his composure and spoke. "I have to go. I'll let Mr. Wellington know you are here. Don't go anywhere now, you hear?"

Liz finally had received her first kiss. It was so beautiful, she took a photo of it with her mind and thought she'd keep it for all time. While daydreaming the nurse called her into the office. After examining her, the nurse said it was nothing more than a bad bruise on her knee. Liz wouldn't need any medication or x-rays. The nurse told Liz to go home and rest. Liz called a cab and headed home.

That evening Liz told Grandma Anta what had occurred. Anta welcomed the idea very much, but wanted Liz to always stay focused on her work. Liz promised that if it were to become a relationship, she would do everything in her power to stay true to her work first.

The home phone rang a little past seven and Grandma Anta answered. Sure enough, it was Rick on the other end wanting to speak with Liz. Liz had butterflies in her stomach and ran to the phone, but cleared her throat and spoke calmly. "Hey, Rick."

Rick spoke, "I didn't have your cell number so I looked you up using Google. Hope you're ok now."

"I'm okay, nothing to worry about, just some bad bruising, no worries," she replied nervously.

"Well, that's good news, I'm happy to hear...well, I mean happy for you, of course!" replied Rick nervously.

Liz caught on and spoke. "Would you like to hang out tomorrow? It is Friday and I was thinking after class, we could get dinner and a movie?" asked Liz as she squinted one eye and thought she had been too direct.

"Ahhh, yes sure, I am free, that would be really great. See you then!" he replied.

Liz had a big smile on her face, and Grandma Anta was doing the happy dance. To Liz, Rick was a boyish man, as if the man inside of the boy was struggling to come out. She loved the way his bubble gum breath smelled. His tongue was sweet, and his cologne was spicy and strong. It was all very seductive, even if the kiss had lasted less than five minutes. It felt as if the universe was conspiring to make love happen between two very shy people. Liz was so excited for her first date with Rick that she could hardly sleep.

Chapter 7

"The circle of life"

Rick and Liz's first date went off without a hitch. The night was a magical one, and they connected on every level. It was a blessing to find out they had much more in common than they thought. Rick walked Liz home that night and spoke about conspiracies. "I love conspiracy theories. I always believed there was more to what we've always been told," he said hoping to get a reaction from Liz.

"Are you stalking my social media wall?" Liz said while chuckling a little.

"Well, what can I do? I wanted to get to know the girl I liked, I was a little…"

"Shy?"

Rick kicked rocks on the pavement with his foot as he looked down on the ground.

"That's alright, I was also shy!" declared Liz.

"It is true though, Liz, conspiracy does fascinate me."

Liz got closer and went for the kill. She kissed him tenderly as he slowly grabbed her in his arms and held her tight. Liz and Rick embraced lovingly. They felt as if they were the only two people in the universe.

Rick returned Liz home around at 10 p.m., and Liz was tired, but not too tired to talk to Grandma Anta. Grandma was up waiting for Liz so she could finally continue her story. Liz opened the door while she waved good bye to Rick, who had now started walking fast down the street heading home.

Grandma Anta was sitting in her rocking chair with a cup of tea in her hands. She had a cup ready for Liz on the coffee table. "Grandma! Hey, you waited up for me," said Liz.

"He looks like a fine gentleman, that Rick. Did you have a good time?"

Liz spoke while she sat down and adjusted her skirt. "I did, he's so smart Grandma. We laughed, shared our meal, and then laughed some more. He's a wonderful guy!"

"I saw that kiss. It's okay, I won't tell your dad. You're almost nineteen. I was married at your age you know. I understand love very well," said Grandma winking Liz's way.

"Oh well, nowadays we just don't know. I'm not looking for marriage, Grandma, I still have a ways to go before I get my degree. Speaking of, how about that story now?"

"Absolutely, you ready?"

Liz smiled and nodded.

Grandma closed her eyes, and began. "The Queen was happy and the King couldn't wait to hold his flesh and blood in hand. Construction had to come to halt. The foundation hadn't even been dug up to its full capacity, as droughts that year were making things unbearable once more. Months went by and the Queen was showing signs of pregnancy more than ever. Things were calm in Egypt, but Khafa was ever so alive and burning with lust for the King.

Khafa often sat with the King and Queen during their council meetings with advisers as they discussed how to proceed next. Jealous looks and heavy stares were ever so evident once more amongst the members. Khafa knew this all too well, but the Queen was blind to it all. The King ignored it and played the part of the politically correct underdog. Khafa knew she had to get to the bottom of every problem, since the King was preoccupied with Egypt and his wife was still behaving badly with whatever time she had left before the baby was due.

So, one day Khafa entered the bathing compound where only men would bathe. Women had their own bathing quarters on the opposite side of the temple. While inside, she spied on two new members whom she had suspected of plotting against the Queen. Khafa made sure no one was around and from where she stood no one would ever see her.

"This dynasty is a travesty to us all! Do they really think; they'll be successful in their projects?" said the first member.

The other spoke while he looked around the room. "Priestess Khafa is evil; she must be stopped!" Khafa's eyes grew bigger at the words spoken, and the other member spoke again. "I'd love to stick it to her real good!" He stuck out his pelvis, and they both laughed like mad men.

Khafa slowly exited the room. She stopped by a nearby pillar to gather her thoughts and took a deep breath. She knew she had a problem on her hands once more and had to rid the realm of such filthy non-believers to the cause. She would have to make their deaths look like an accident. She gathered cobra snakes from the desert and with the help of her assistants, the ones who were faithful to her alone, venom was drawn into a small capsule bottle. Once the bottle was full, the snakes were released back into the wilderness and her plan was set into motion.

Arriving that night to his private quarters, the first evil man stripped his attire and headed for bed, when he found Khafa there naked and seducing him with her body. "Khafa! How did you get in here?" the man asked.

Khafa knew the outside of his quarters were always heavily guarded. "Come to me, that's not important now. I've been watching you, and I desire you in me," she replied with lust in her eyes. Her breast had been exposed and called for his touch. The man couldn't help but be under her spell and jumped into bed beside her. He had the biggest smile a man could have, because this was a dream come true for him. Every man in the temple wanted to be with Khafa. He was rock hard with desire, and Khafa rolled her eyes as he entered her. But his bad breath was foul, so she pushed him off of her as if she had been playing a game and spoke. "A little drink before, we continue? It'll make things fun and mysterious!"

The man nodded in approval as she poured the wine for him. The poison sat at the bottom of the glass already, and she mixed it while he turned away to get comfortable. She handed him the chalice and spoke again, "Men first." The man was smitten by her charm and then she poured her glass, and they began drinking. He gulped the wine quickly, as he was too excited to waste any more time. Khafa smiled a little, exposing her pearly white teeth.

"You are so sexy and beautiful, come lay beside me," he said.

"Drink up, all of it and I'll do whatever you like." The man drank even quicker. Soon his breathing was heavy and excessive sweat oozed out of his pores. Khafa knew the venom was working its way to his heart, and there was no stopping it. The man was still operating and doing fine, so she went down on him to kill some time before he entered her again.

This one is a tough one to kill, she thought as she performed oral sex. By now he was starting to become dizzy, so she poured him another glass and added more venom, emptying her bottle. "Here drink some more. We're having fun aren't we?" she asked. Khafa laughed wickedly, and the man became confused. As he started to convulse, Khafa stood on top of him and spoke, "There is no place amongst us, if you are not a believer!" The man started to yell for help, but Khafa took a pillow to silence his screams and spoke once more. "Have a safe journey to the afterlife!" In the blink of an eye, he lay dead. Khafa had no remorse as she removed the pillow from his face, wiped his mouth clean, turned him over and placed a blanket on his body.

She dressed herself and exited the quarters from the back that lead to a court yard. She fled the scene undetected and undisturbed. The morning after he was found, no one knew what happened, and Khafa never spoke a word to anyone about it. The Queen thought his heart had stopped; after all, he wasn't very young.

Khafa's plan had worked so well, she longed for more. The other member wasn't as inviting, since he preferred the company of men. Unable to use her body or charms on him, she would have to try a different plan and perhaps secure the help of her assistants.

Another month passed and the Queen was now in labor. Khafa and her priestesses attended the birth and did a ceremonial ritual before the Queen. Khafa knew this baby hadn't a great chance at life due to the fact that it was born early. In fact, the Queen had given birth to stillborn baby.

The King screamed out in anguish when he saw the child and blamed the Queen for its death. Khafa ran to the King after he stormed out, leaving the Queen with a dead infant in her arms. The King cried heavily in Khafa's arms. "A boy it was, the heir to the throne. The Gods have punished me, why?" he asked.

Khafa held him tighter in her arms, but he refused to be held like a baby and broke free. "This is because I love another. I have no honor for my bride. I am sure of this," said the King in despair.

Khafa nodded in disapproval. "No. my King, it's nature's way. You have done nothing wrong!" But, the King cried even harder and walked away, leaving Khafa in her own tears.

Three months after the death of the future Pharaoh, the Queen was once again pregnant. It hadn't taken them long as her womb was still young and healthy, and they were both very serious about having children. Khafa hadn't forgotten about her project, the project that kept being delayed and delayed by the King and the droughts. Now, it was time for her next move.

The next evening Khafa and her servants approached the other councilman who plotted against her. Khafa's ranking within the palace was much more than other high priestesses, and she was well-protected at all times. Even the King let her do as she pleased. She had summoned him for a business dinner, and the man was happy to attend.

When he arrived, several lovely young men greeted him. The man was in heaven, but then again everything Khafa did was with taste and extravagance. The councilman sat at the appointed table and said, "To what do I owe this lovely meal before me?" Khafa caught the double meaning and smirked. She spoke as the young men used giant palm leaves to fan their seated guest. "I understand you have power of the fishery on the Nile." She paused to wait for an answer.

He finally said, "I most certainly do. We've been successful in every aspect. The King favors me as the keeper of such."

Khafa thought him to be a fool and hadn't cared that much about his success with the King and the fishery business. "Yes, well, I invite you to our new boat. We would love to have your blessings. She is splendid and having you aboard would be for entertainment and approval, of course. We wouldn't want to tread the Nile without your consent." She spoke charmingly and began to rub her hands up and down the leg of one of the young men. The man smiled and sat back on his chair while another helper asked him if he'd like his shoulders rubbed. The man invited him to go lower, so the younger man reached around to accommodate his elder.

"What is it that you seek, my priestess?" asked the man breathing heavy now.

Khafa raised an eyebrow and said, "I seek your blessing and company, that is all." The helper pulled himself away so he could pour the man some more wine.

"Forgive me, my priestess, but it is your duty to bless all, with your rituals and incantations. You and I have never really enjoyed one another's company, so it is only fair I ask," he said.

Khafa once sent yet another speechless message to the helper. Soon the young man was kissing and embracing the councilman. More wine was being poured and the man was enchanted by Khafa's set up. Khafa could see that boys were his weakness. He finally agreed to be her guest the next day at noon.

Khafa wondered why he had been a little reluctant, so she had her helpers watch his every move that night. He and some lovers had taken some time by the Nile that night engaging in orgies and fun. The boys pushed him into the river, but he refused to go further than his waist, and yelled, "I can't swim!" Now Khafa knew why he had been afraid to be a guest. It was an unusual thing to for a sailor and keeper of the fishery not to be able to swim, and now her new plan was established.

The King had drunk an excessive amount of wine that night, and was flirtatious with the young, beautiful women. Khafa wasn't amused by this, but the Queen had taken an early dismissal to her quarters for she had been feeling excessively tired already. Watching the King in his quarters with those women infuriated Khafa. When he saw Khafa watching him, he purposely began kissing an attractive young priestess and fondling another's breasts. He knew this would make her jealous and furious. Khafa walked away in tears. He laughed like a demon and the voice that carried over made her shut her eyes tightly and walk away even faster still. The King was becoming a brute and the love he felt for Khafa was slowly fading."

Liz yawned and looked at the clock. "Wow! Grandma, it's midnight and I need to go to bed!" Grandma agreed and they both said their goodnights.

Liz awoke to the sound of her parents lugging their suitcases up the stairs. A red eye flight from Berlin had them jet lagged and hungry.

"Mom, Dad!" Liz yelled as she ran to hug her parents. Liz then told her parents she had been on a date with Rick. Her father wasn't too receptive to the news, but he trusted his nineteen-year-old daughter.

Catherine was happy but as always she did her usual scolding. "Education first! Got it!"

"Yes, Mother!" Liz responded as she rolled her eyes.

Breakfast was ready for all. Grandma had cooked up a feast for their arrival. As Grandma served up the meal, she said, "Lizzy needs to learn how to cook. She has a boyfriend now!"

"Stop that, he's not my fiancé, well...not yet!"

Everyone in the room laughed.

Liz danced around her room that day, cleaning and studying and then cleaning some more. She checked her iPhone, hoping to receive a message from Sticks, when she instead saw a text from Rick.

Hey beautiful, just taking a moment to say hello!

Well, hello sir! :)

I'm studying for Monday's exam, I'll be doing the   same

tomorrow, would you like to study together, here or my house?

Liz, you there?

Yes! Sorry, I think it's best you come here.

Yes, sure no problem; I'll be there at one? Is that okay?

Absolutely! ;)

See you then!

Liz's heart was pounding again. She searched her closet for the perfect outfit to wear the next day.

***

Studying together had been great; they connected on every level. Catherine and Justin took a liking to Rick, as did Grandma Anta. After seven hours, Rick said good-bye to Liz's family, and Liz walked him to the porch. Before he left, Rick kissed her on the lips. Liz naturally shook like a leaf, and Rick made sure she was comfortable by placing his arms around her. "I guess this makes it official then!"

Liz smiled and knew exactly what he meant. "Yes, I agree!"

"I like you very much Liz. Good night, Beautiful!" said Rick as he walked away. He looked back again when he reached the corner and Liz waved good-bye. Those butterflies churning in her belly at the sound of the word "beautiful" made her heart smile. Content and happy, Liz went to sleep peacefully.

The March weather was breezy and balmy, like Liz's life had become. School was a slice of pie, and Liz's grades were great. She and Rick had begun studying excessively for their finals. Rick was a tower of knowledge and opened up a whole new world for Liz. She was becoming a woman, as Rick was becoming a man. It was perhaps because they complimented each other very well.

Their union was a blessed one because they had both been very serious in their approach toward school. Their grades proved it time after time. That fall, Rick planned a very romantic dinner for Liz at his house, while his parents were away for the weekend.

There was a little chill in the November air, but it didn't stopped Rick from making the perfect outdoor setting for Liz. That evening, thousands of stars illuminated the sky. Rick handed Liz a poncho and pulled a chair so she could sit comfortably. Tiny white lights covered the trees in Rick's backyard, and soft music was playing in the distance. He had prepared two covered meals with silver tops, and white wine was being chilled in the ice bucket. Rick had gone the distance for her, and it was evident they both knew where this would lead. "You've out done yourself Rick; this place is majestic. I want to thank you for such a lovely setting."

"Liz, it's my pleasure and this house is ours for the night. I'm glad you like it. Here...let me pour you some wine," said Rick. Liz had tried wine on a number of occasions with Grandma Anta, and Rick remembered that white wine was her favorite. She extended her glass willingly and let the ambrosia flow. Liz remembered Grandma Anta's story when Khafa poured the wine in the chalice for the council member and couldn't help but laugh.

Rick smiled and asked, "Already drunk?"

Liz laughed even harder. "It's a funny thing, Grandma has been telling me a story of ancient Egypt, of a lost dynasty and her Khemitian background, since I was eleven. The story is ongoing, since so many things happened in between. We never got to the end really, and wine played a big part in one particular story."

Rick smiled. "*Ahhhh*, sheer coincidence! Let me guess, someone poisoned someone with too much wine?" added the brilliant Rick.

Liz's eyes widened at his comment and spoke again. "Yeah! Something like that, very close to that actually!"

"*Hmmm*, just an educated guess on my part. Poison was used often, because it was undetectable and a sure, slow killer!" replied Rick.

Liz dug into her dish and so did Rick. It was a delectable meal of fish, cooked up by Rick and his mother before Ricks parents left for the weekend. They ate baked scampi, red snapper, baked potatoes, string green beans and a lovely mixed salad. These were Liz's favorite foods and made Liz melt, as Rick remembered every detail of all she liked.

After the meal, Liz felt a little tipsy because she drank two glasses of wine. They danced close together under the starry sky, and Liz could feel Rick's manhood grow as they swayed to the music. Liz whispered, "I love you, Rick."

"I love you too, my Pharaoh." It was their first "I love you," moment after many months of playing "hard to get game." It was real and beautiful. Liz let her guard down and finally gave into her desire for Rick. Liz coaxed Rick up to his bedroom, and Rick followed willingly.

Liz shut the door behind her and drew Rick to her. They gazed into each other's eyes and Liz spoke. "You will be the first."

"I'd also love to be the last," Rick said softly.

Liz smiled and thought this to be so romantic, she then undressed Rick slowly while Rick did the same to her. Rick sighed at the beauty of Liz's untouched and virgin body; he thought he was the luckiest guy in the world that night. Liz let him touch her gently and fondle her breasts. Rick's male part was evidently growing before her. Liz gazed upon it and moved her hand down his firm stomach to his groin. Her touch was firm, but not hurtful. Rick was in paradise, and Liz could feel the shivers running down his spine.

Rick slowly moved toward the bed and laid her down. He mounted her gently and Liz started to moan. She was ready more than ever when he began sucking on her nipples. She stopped him and pleaded. "Now, take me, all of me!"

Rick entered her slowly as she held on to the bed sheets, and moaned from the very core of her body. Rick was pleasurable, sexy and romantic all at once. Liz began to enjoy herself as the pain subsided.

Liz had the right moves; she was a natural with her love moves. Rick tried to hold back, but they both reached orgasmic heights simultaneously. Liz let out the biggest moan ever that opened up the portal for Rick to join her. It was wonderful, exciting and surprising. Liz was one of the lucky ones to have it mostly her way. They held each other tightly in bed and Liz spoke, "I can't believe I waited this long!"

Rick laughed and said, "Better this way, I guess. I loved it Liz."

Liz gazed into his eyes and her heart melted once more, and she mounted him unexpectedly. Rick was game for another round, but this time it was to be more aggressive. She pinned his arms down, kissed his neck and torso all over and then began taking him in her mouth. Holding nothing back, she rode him gracefully, the thrusts from her pelvis in sync with him. A wonderful evening had turned into a perfect evening when they lay in each other's arms for hours laughing and giggling after two magical love making sessions. Rick said, "I took you honorably the first time, the second was all your doing. I hope you'll stick around. You make me a better person Liz," He declared his undying love for her.

Liz said, "Please don't break my heart. I could never bear it!"

"All I can do is try," he replied.

Then Liz dressed as Rick watched her. Her body was curvy, and her breasts were huge. It was obvious to Liz that Rick loved every inch of her. She knew he liked her hair, which hugged her voluptuous hips.

Finally, the romance came to halt for the time being. It was after two a.m., so Rick drove Liz home. They sat in the car for a few minutes and talked. "Liz, I want to say something. I think it's important," said Rick. Liz sat very still as she listened.

"I got a job at the local museum. It's a part time gig for now. I'm almost 21, so I have plans to move out. I have enough money saved from my part time job at McDonald's. I hope this doesn't change anything between us. I wanted to tell you earlier, but tonight was your night."

Liz was ecstatic at the news and felt compelled to lean over and kiss Rick. "This will never change anything. I love it, I love you, and I know some day you'll be the greatest archeologist ever. Whatever makes you happy, makes me happy!" she said with a sparkle in her eye.

Rick let out a sigh of relief. Liz laughed and said, "Oh c'mon! Don't tell me you were nervous. That's not what I experienced in the bedroom tonight!"

"What you saw tonight was just the beginning!" said Rick showing his macho side. Liz chuckled and before she said good night, they kissed one last time.

Liz entered her bedroom and threw herself on her bed and sighed as she recapped all the events that night. She loved the feeling of love-making and wanted more. She couldn't wait to be with Rick the next day, if time allowed.

A knock at the door that morning woke Liz from her wonderful dreams. She slowly opened one eye, and saw Grandma Anta standing in the doorway.

"It's late, you must have been really tired to sleep in so late," said Grandma Anta who had her hands behind her back as if she was holding something. "It's after 11 o'clock!"

"What do you have there?" asked Liz, ignoring Grandma's comment.

"Here, these came for you, just minutes ago!" Grandma Anta had a smile on her face so wide it revealed her dentures all too well. A bouquet of fresh cut red roses, all twelve beautifully bunched up with a note attached to the bow holding it together.

Liz smiled and opened the note. She read the contents out loud. "For my Nefertiti this a.m. Thank you for the best night of my life. Always yours, Rick." Liz's heart melted again.

Grandma Anta frowned. "You did the deed last night, didn't you?"

Liz denied it, but then Grandma Anta spoke. "I will never tell your father. As long as you love each other, it's okay. Don't be embarrassed, it's natural!"

Liz nodded in approval, but really hadn't had the heart to go into details.

"I can only say one thing! I told you so!" said Grandma.

Liz was confused as to what she meant. "What do you mean?"

"You do look like Nefertiti, and this young man is deeply in love with you. You have my blessings, for whatever lies ahead!"

Liz smiled and hugged her Grandma tightly. "I know what I want this morning Grandma, more than anything, for the time being," said Liz.

Grandma knew exactly what she meant. "Indeed! The story! Back to Egypt this morning!"

Before Grandma began her story, Liz sat up in bed and said, "Wait Grandma! I must text Rick and say thank you for the flowers."

Rick answered Liz's text right away and invited her to go bowling that evening. Liz accepted the invitation, Grandma waiting patiently as the two lovebirds texted back and forth.

When Liz put her phone down and settled back onto her bed, Grandma said, "Well, finally, you have time for your old Grandma. I hope you enjoy this part of the story. So, as I said the last time, Khafa patiently waited with her crew of helpers, and assistants on the harbor of the Nile that day for the councilman to make his way to the boat of lust waiting for him.

Khafa had once again out did herself, by adding platters of grapes, exotic fruits, dates and all the wine one man could drink. The beautiful looking young men were ready for action as well. They had been in the company of men, and some of the men were of a higher ranking in blood lines and therefore more desirable to men of the council, not like those free loading peasants he had swam with the night before. It was to make his senses even more warped and unaware of what was coming.

The councilman appeared and excused his tardiness. "*Ahhhh* Khafa, apologies on my behalf, I was caught up in some business, and I could not break away!" he said entering the boat at full speed.

Khafa spoke, "Apologies accepted, do not worry, please, enjoy!" She had an evil smirk on her face but no one had seen that. The councilman looked around. Oddly enough, the young men had been attracted to the councilman and wanted to have him. They had no notion of what was to take place there that day. They were given a free pass to a sexual escapade, and a refusal to such entertainment was unheard of. Only Khafa's closest assistant was fully aware of what really was going on.

After minutes of treading the Nile, the councilman wasted no time in getting acquainted with the homosexual help. He was poured wine in a chalice, fed grapes by those he fondled, and two helpers went down on him as he moaned in sheer happiness proclaiming, "Now this is the life!"

Khafa stood there watching the sex fest. Nothing was hidden back then. The royals and their panels always had sex openly. After a while, Khafa's assistant coaxed her into a stroll to the back of the boat. "It is time," he whispered.

Khafa said, "Not now, let him enjoy himself before he meets the hand of death." She walked back to the front of the boat and waited another half hour.

By that point, the councilman entered a young helper from behind. The boat was magnificent, and it was clear that the councilman always had pleasure before business and sometimes during. When he looked up at Khafa, he spoke in between his groans. "Isn't he beautiful, look at him, those pink lips around my cock. And that sweet tongue of warmth. You know how to pick them, my dear Khafa!"

Khafa smiled. "I'm glad you enjoyed yourself, there are more if you like, our time isn't limited here. We have all day."

"Indeed, I shall be here all day and get my fill, now...for business."

Khafa knew they were well into the deep part of the Nile and away from the bustling city now, so she summoned another young man to follow them as they strolled to the back of the boat. Khafa carefully showed off the boat and Khafa's assistant followed right behind her.

"It is a swell boat; you've done well. My blessings to you and this boat," he offered. As he continued to inspect the boat, Khafa looked towards her assistant and nodded. Her assistant reached over and pushed the councilman off the boat! Khafa waited 'til the music up front would be loud enough so no one would hear the councilman's screams in the water. The boat was sailing away and Khafa waved good-bye as the councilman drowned.

No one was to be trusted except her assistant Azet.

Khafa knew she had to kill the others as well, and so a slaughter fest had begun that day on the boat. Many bodies were thrown overboard. The ship sailed with originally 10 men aboard and only two made their way home--Khafa and Azet, of course.

Arriving at the harbor later that evening, they found that the King had been searching high and low for the Councilman Ahmud. When he ran into Khafa, he spoke with a concerned look. "Have you seen, our councilman Ahmud?"

Khafa started to worry that he would be found. "No, my King. I haven't. You know Ahmud, he's probably off on some sexual adventure. I'm sure he'll turn up soon," she replied.

"Yes, indeed!" replied the King, knowing Ahmud's ways.

Khafa left the King's side only to bump into the pregnant Queen before her. "Khafa, greetings," said Aketu.

"Greetings, my Queen. I hope you are in better spirits today."

"Indeed I am, after losing our son and now pregnant again, and a promise of love. It is a fine day!"

"Love?"

"Yes, the King and I have decided that the gods would favor our child, if we were to really love each other, it is for the best."

Khafa sighed silently and took a deep breath, speaking again with a heavy heart, "I wish this for you, my Queen; your happiness is essential."

The Queen looked at her with suspicion for she had seen the hurt in her eyes.

Khafa

Khafa began to walk away as a tear fell from her eye. It took every ounce of strength to conceal her shattered heart.

The Queen grabbed her arm to whisper in her ear, "He's mine, forget him."

Khafa nodded, ran to her private quarters, and pushed her guards aside to let her in. She slammed the door and fell to her knees. She had lost her one true love and cried hysterically. Murder and losses were on her hands, and if that wasn't enough, Khafa set other plans in motion to rebel against this love. A quiet war was to commence.

Khafa wondered how the Queen knew of their relationship. Did she see them? Had they been caught? And why did the Queen spare her life? Was the Queen waiting for the right moment to rid herself of Khafa for good? It was all overwhelming, but Khafa knew she had to be careful at all times. Aketu spared Khafa's life for the time being because she had helped the Queen in troubled times, but Khafa was skating on thin ice now, and so she sought the company of men that night for her own needs.

This new dynasty wasn't like any other. Khafa started resenting the fact she ever brought the Prince there to be made King. He had become distant, unapproachable, greedy and unfaithful to Khafa. The worst part was that Khafa let it happen. Consumed by power, Khafa overlooked everything else and dug fearlessly into her schemes and plots that were ever so successful. Being evil was so easy, she had forgotten what it was like to be good. Khafa also knew that love couldn't be sparked with just words. A deep connection had to be made, and she laughed away the hours in the company of men, as she was sure she'd always be the King's real love no matter what anyone said. Her confidence was resurfacing more than ever before, and her opportunity to test him would come to pass soon enough.

Liz interrupted Grandma and said, "I'm hungry, would you like to go get something to eat today? My treat!" Liz had never taken her Grandma out before and thought she would spend some of her hard earned money from helping Dad out at the shop.

"Sure, I don't mind McDonald's, haven't had that in a long time!"

***

Liz was now getting older and a part time job was in the cards she thought. Dad wasn't fond of her working outside the family, so he offered her Thursday nights and Friday nights after classes, and every other Saturday. Those hours were perfect as Rick had similar hours, and they would meet up afterwards or before their shifts.

Liz had now turned 20, and Rick had popped the question! The question of living together. Rick was a responsible young man, and his tiny apartment was neat and tidy. He paid his bills on time and managed to save money as well.

The Hawann's threw an annual party in their backyard that year and Justin approached Rick. "When were you going to tell me?"

Rick looked confused and spoke, "I'm sorry Mr. Hawann, I don't follow?"

"About asking Liz to move in with you?"

"Oh, yes, well..."

Justin interrupted in mid-sentence. "We've known for a little while now. I overheard Liz on the phone with you. She's afraid to let us down and she should be!"

After a long pause, Justin spoke again, "Catherine and I are in agreement, but, if you hurt her, just once, you better pray that I'm not alive to see it!"

Rick nodded and ran to tell Liz the good news. Liz ran to her dad and gave him the biggest hug ever. "Dad! Thank you, are you sure?"

"Yes! Now get out of here both of you before I change my mind!"

Before she left, Liz reassured Grandma that she would stop by every day for supper because Rick worked long hours at the museum during the week. Liz was a little nervous about moving out, because cooking wasn't exactly her thing. She could clean house very well, but she would learn recipes over time and attempt to make a decent meal once in a while.

The relationship was bliss. Liz learned responsibility through Rick. He cared about living the right way and doing no wrong. These were the features that Justin loved and respected dearly about the young man.

Liz and Rick were on the verge of graduating. Even though Rick was two years older, he had a late start in his classes because of some confusion after high school. He didn't attend college right away, he waited a few years. Working full time at McDonald's had taught him a lesson about hard work. Rick was happy he went to college because it brought him to Liz.

Liz had done well on her promise to visit Grandma and her parents every day. She found the time between work and school to make the visits count with Grandma especially, for her parents would often be at work.

Rick began working for the museum full time as a guide, McDonald's was done and a bigger and better salary was the works for Rick.

Liz visited one Saturday afternoon. "Grandma! I'm here!" she exclaimed as she made her way through the backyard and into the back house. Grandma jumped up for joy when she saw Liz and started a hug fest.

"Lizzy, can I get you a coffee? Or some food?" asked Grandma with a twinkle in her eye.

"Nahhh. Grandma, I'm good, had a coffee on the way over. How you doing? Everything ok?" she asked.

"I'm fine, I just miss you very much, Lizzy!" replied Grandma Liz hugged her again.

"I'm doing well. How is school going?"

"I'll be graduating soon; hope you can make the ceremony."

"Wouldn't miss it for the world!" Stubborn old Grandma still managed to make coffee and bring over some sweet delights to the table and Liz smiled. "How is everything with Rick?" asked the curious Anta.

Liz spoke with that twinkle of love in her eye. "It's great Grandma. He's taught me so much about living responsibly, and we get along just fine."

Grandma smiled and said, "Good, stick to those you can learn from and speaking of which...you ready for more of Egypt?"

"You know it! Shoot!"

Chapter 8

"A new age"

"An event was in place for the King's birthday that late July in Egypt, and Khafa sought out other means of testing the will of the King. She opened the event with her usual rituals and the priestesses followed. The King loved her dance moves once again. He was intoxicated by her, and Khafa knew what she was doing. The Queen hadn't been so ecstatic as she watched her husband enjoy the dance and clap harder than anyone, and even getting up to give the priestesses a standing ovation.

The Queen was starting to have feelings for the King, since her pregnancy had been going really well after her second trimester. The King was receptive to her love or so it seemed.

That night Khafa brought a man to the celebration and introduced him as her husband to be. She danced seductively all around him. He was devilishly handsome, and his body was lean and buffed. He had light brown eyes with tones of yellow and green in them, and his hair was sleek and very dark. He seemed to be into Khafa very much. There was visible lust and sexual tension between them. This made the King furious, because the King was indeed still in love with Khafa, which she had noticed all too well. Her plan to get the King back was working.

Khafa strung her supposed fiancé around in her deep web of lies for a few weeks. She seduced him from near and far, but they had never had sexual intercourse as of yet. She held off to make it look like she was waiting for the consummation to take place after they had been married. He was a priest and so her efforts and declaration of marriage to everyone was justified. He was a priest no one really cared for, hidden amongst the many that served the dynasty, but he was quiet and humble.

Khafa knew how to choose her victims; she had a natural ability to spot the underdog and the weak. The priest was much younger than the King. Khafa liked them that way. Khafa brought the priest before the King, and they both bowed. Khafa said, "My Pharaoh, ruler of Egypt and the afterlife, let me have the pleasure of introducing my future husband." The priest smiled at this declaration as he had been deeply in love already with Khafa.

The Queen was ecstatic by the news, for this meant that Khafa had finally moved on and would let her have her husband's heart all to herself. The King looked down on them with an eyebrow raised and spoke, "This is wonderful news, welcome my priest." The King was in anguish as he looked on Khafa with confused eyes. Khafa smirked evilly and bowed before the King.

The Queen spoke. "Wonderful, indeed. When is the wedding?"

"After the baby is born, my Queen. I will honor your joy first," Khafa replied as the King sat there fuming. Khafa smiled an evil smile, while the Queen personally congratulated the priest, whose name was Satketh.

Satketh and Khafa left the King and Queen's side to mingle among the crowd, but Khafa watched the King closely as he stared her down with evil eyes. At that moment she excused herself, leaving Satketh with other priestesses and priests. Khafa knew the King would follow and sure enough he did. She began running and he picked up the pace 'til he reached her, grabbed her and pinned her on temple wall. They both were out of breath as the King held her firmly making sure no one was around.

"What do you think you're doing?" asked the King with a heavy heart, twisting her wrists behind her back.

"Let go of me. I'm moving on!" she screamed as tears filled her eyes.

The King said, "You are my property forever. You will never marry that man. I forbid it as your King." She started screaming and he covered his free hand When she calmed down, he let her speak.

"You are my King, but I need to be happy, as you are, now...let go of me!" she said as tears fell down her reddened cheeks. The King let her go, then gazed upon her lovingly. Khafa gazed in his eyes that spoke of his undying love, the love he was too proud to declare with words. "You need to love your Queen if you don't want your children to be doomed. Let me be. I'm not your property, not anymore."

Khafa

Khafa composed herself and left the King behind to reflect on his actions. Khafa had been a little confused, but now she knew his love had never stopped. It only died down. His flame was burning at full force now, which was exactly what Khafa wanted. She would continue this game until the King could bear no more.

Finally, when the King had had enough, he made love to her, alone in her chambers, to show her how much he really did still love her. This was the moment Khafa had been waiting for.

It happened one evening as she returned to her chambers. The king was sitting in her chair when she entered the room. She was frightened for a minute but then spoke, "My King." She bowed before his knees.

He gently took her hand and said, "Get up, never bow before me in private, there is no need." Khafa still knelt to show how distant she had become. He had been a stranger to her bed for over a year now. The King then pushed Khafa toward him and held her closely and spoke in her ear. "Your scent is unforgettable, your body is perfection and your lips are sweeter than honey, how did I fail you? How could I ever!" The King began sobbing in Khafa's arms.

"You haven't failed me, I've failed you, my love!" Khafa began to undress before the King as he stood there quietly adoring her bountiful breasts and curves. The King was hard in anticipation, remembering the first time he ever entered her, and this alone made him kiss her passionately. She was desirable and inviting. He threw her across the bed and mounted her. Her legs reached the top of his back, and she locked his body down as they rolled in the bed sheets together without a care. He entered her time and time again that night, and she moaned louder than ever. He was her perfect sexual match. Khafa had many others, but no one was like the King.

The King was clear on her marriage not going through. He forbade it and meant every word. "You must never cross me in this fashion, see it done," he commanded after he had dressed.

Khafa begged him to stay, but he refused. "I must retire to my Queen now. She'll be wondering where I've been. She doesn't dare ask, but lately she has been clinging to me as if I were her last hope," he said.

Khafa grew worried as another obstacle was in the way, the envy of the jealous Queen. "Very well, go," said Khafa walking away, but the King swung her around to meet him face to face.

"It is you I love, never forget," he said as they kissed passionately. Khafa fell to the mercy of his love. He had enslaved her heart, and she was weak for him. It was a twisted love affair, one that would have him sitting as the Alpha and Omega at all times, and she was really nothing but his property to do with what he liked, whenever he desired. He had been extremely jealous and possessive of all he held dear, except for the Queen, his wife. He really didn't care for her and had just strung her along, giving her false hopes time after time, pretending he loved her, while she begged for his real love in return.

Then Prince Takenreh the Second was born. The healthy baby boy came into the world on a late September morning, and Khafa as usual assisted the birth. The people were rejoicing and content, for the King and Queen had finally been successful in producing an heir, an heir so perfect he was loved by all. The Queen was thankful to Khafa and all her efforts. Hieroglyphics depicting the young Prince, were chiseled all over the Kingdom. He was a fine boy indeed, and the King was ever so proud of the child he had helped create.

Khafa loved the boy as her own as time went on. He had been growing at an alarming rate and had now begun walking. The Queen favored Khafa to watch over him at all times when the Queen couldn't. It was another duty placed upon her by the King and Queen that she could not refuse.

Khafa's plan for her project was once again being tossed under the rug. There were too many droughts and floods to continue with this major undertaking. With the King on her side now more than ever, she would take the opportunity to put this into motion. So, Khafa talked the King into calling a council meeting about her project once more and he had agreed. The Queen looked uninterested that morning in the council meeting, and many members had agreed that Egypt had no financial means to take up the project again. While Egypt was doing well, she couldn't sustain the project yet. In a vote the council decided that Khafa's project would be considered the following year.

Khafa wasn't satisfied with their decision. She formally addressed the King and Queen. "My King, my Queen, we have put this plan into action before. If we had continued the floods would have never covered the area completely. We cannot afford to let this sit. We can raise the money, if we raise the taxes on the land," she said with much conviction.

The King hadn't said a word, yet three council members stood up and argued. "Raise the taxes! You are pretentious and misguided!" said the first council member.

"She is the whore of the King; of course, she may be so bold!" said the second member, and the third one nodded in approval. The room stood quiet. Khafa couldn't believe the words the man had just said. The Queen was furious and asked her helpers to take her and the baby back to her chambers.

The room was in a state of chaos, while Khafa yelled at the top of her lungs. "How dare you!"

Then the king stood up and yelled, "Order, order in the council, immediately!" He was terrifying when he yelled, and Khafa ran out of the meeting with tears in her eyes. Khafa was just like the rest of them, an object to be used, she thought. She would have to make another plot to remove more members one by one, but what would that solve? They seemed to have found haters for the project time and time again. The addition and removal of council members, all back stabbing liars, would be futile.

Khafa stayed in her quarters that night awaiting the King. When she heard the expected knock, she ran to the door expecting to see the King, but it was, the Queen.

"My Queen, please, enter," said Khafa uneasily.

"You have crossed the line once more, like I knew you would, have you no conscience?" asked the Queen hastily.

"The King is to have many lovers, my Queen. He may also have many wives, if he chooses too. It's the new era, you are no stranger to this," she replied with confidence.

The Queen grew angry at her statement. "Love is not an option. It was our right to practice it as such. He swore an oath to me long ago when I was Pharaoh!" she said.

Khafa spoke boldly. "Yes, an oath of no love between you, but I see you make the rules up as you go along!"

"You have shamed us, and now everyone will know. When this gets out, we will lose our credibility amongst all!" The guards stood beside the Queen, and Khafa grew worried.

Then the Queen yelled, "Take her to the torture chamber; she will be charged with adultery!" The Queen was out of her mind completely, and Khafa struggled in the arms of the guards as they roughly held her.

"Adultery? You are insane? The King will never agree to this, do you hear me!" The guards dragged her kicking and screaming across the temple to a dismal chamber where prisoners were held with chains by their wrists. Khafa was chained up quickly and then left alone in puddle of her tears.

The Queen knew she was too weak to win the game of love with her King, and she was consumed by jealousy and crushing Khafa. What did Khafa have that she didn't? It was hurtful to her pride and especially her ego. Khafa was repeatedly tortured that night by the request of the Queen. She had been beaten severely, and raped by the guards until she passed out.

The next morning, she awoke and could barely see. Where was her King? And why hadn't he come to rescue her? She thought of all the good she ever brought the Queen. How could she have done such a despicable thing? After everything she did lovingly for the dynasty? The Queen was an ungrateful, spoiled bitch, she thought, and once she made her way out of here, she would be quiet, obedient and disconnected from it all. Bleeding from the wounds on her knees, rib cage and back, Khafa lay on the floor next to the rats that ran all about her cell. Her soul was dying with her. Whatever good she had left in her was gone. Her tears now stung her bruised eyes.

Suddenly a man approached the cell, and Khafa ran to the corner in fear. "Khafa!" whispered the man. Khafa recognized that voice all too well. It was Satketh.

Khafa ran to his side and spoke. "Satketh, leave now before they see you!" Satketh stood there without words when he saw Khafa's face.

"I searched for you high and low. I knew they took you here when your priestesses mentioned it to me. The King isn't here, he left on business for a few days," said Satketh knowing he was the only one who could free her from the chains.

Khafa now knew why the Queen had been in such a hurry. She wanted to carry out her plan without the King being present. She also knew the Queen would free her just before his arrival. She would have everyone in the Kingdom silenced, like it never took place, just to teach Khafa a lesson. "Very well, I will sleep with the rats for the time being. I know it is temporary, thank you Satketh for informing me," she said.

Satketh spoke again. "I'm sorry for your pain. Know that I will always care for you. Here take some bread, I know they aren't feeding you much here." He handed her a morsel and she devoured it quickly. "The guards will come again, be strong!" he said and exited the temple without being seen.

Khafa laughed hysterically when Satketh left. Someone cared for her after all, but her laugh was mainly because the Queen outsmarted her and had done it so carefully. The beatings had stopped, but rape was inevitable. The Queen had ordered the beatings to stop in order to allow time for the wounds to heal, another brilliant move. When the King came back, he wouldn't notice anything.

After five days had passed, and the bruises were fading, another visitor came to her side. "Well, what a sight for sore eyes you are!" said the councilman. Khafa stared straight ahead and didn't speak. "It is funny how a woman so powerful in Egypt today, ends up here, what have you done?" he asked sarcastically. Khafa still refused to speak. "If you won't speak that is fine with me, just know this. You are being stopped by a stronger force, and you will never see your project through, no matter how many members you rid yourself of," he said and then walked away.

The High Priestess

Khafa's eyes grew wide at the words spoken. What did he know? And who and what was this force behind the scenes? Soon after the Queen came, and said, "Khafa my priestess, you are being freed, but know that you no longer have the luxury of my husband's heart. This is your second warning. You will continue your services with us as usual. Your chambers await."

Khafa spoke carefully. "Yes my Queen, thank you." Khafa walked away to a breezy moonlit sky and soaked up the air while the Queen cried quietly in the cell. The Queen wasn't heartless on that night. Khafa ran back to her freedom that night, but she bathed in the priestesses' quarters to wash away the dirt and grime on her skin. The herbs and medicine would help her recovery in days to come.

The accusation of adultery was never pursued. It was only to scare Khafa off and it had worked well. On the third day after her release, the King visited Khafa's compound where all the priestesses resided. They were working hard making potions and incantations. Khafa saw the King drawing closer to her and now worry set in. Khafa had to think up a storm of excuses to fend him off.

"*Ahhhh*, Khafa my beauty. I have missed you so!" said the King.

"My King, welcome back," she said as she bowed before him.

The King was all smiles and happy to be back home. "Won't you visit me tonight?" he whispered.

"I would love to my King, but I'm not feeling so well," she replied.

"Well, fair enough, I shall see you tomorrow then!" the King said insistently.

Khafa knew she had a problem once again. Racing through the palace, Khafa searched for the Queen so she could make her aware. Finding Aketu in the bathing quarters with her helpers washing her body, Khafa asked the helpers to leave. The Queen snapped her fingers and the helpers left. "My Queen, sorry for the interruption. I'll have you know the King came to see me, just minutes ago."

The Queen frowned. "What does he seek? Doesn't he ever have enough?" asked the Queen.

Khafa

Khafa spoke again. "Know that it doesn't come from me. You will have to tell him yourself. I told him I was not feeling well, but he will never understand. He will punish me if I tell him I no longer love him. Please, my Queen, I have had enough. Won't you spare me more punishment?"

The Queen saw she was genuine and feared for her life and then spoke. "Fair enough, I will tell him. Go now and stay far away until I have a moment with him alone."

Khafa thanked the Queen and headed back to her compound. Khafa would give up her love for the King. To go back to the life of misery she once held was out of the question, especially after gaining such power among the nation's finest.

Liz interrupted Grandma; almost two hours had gone by. "Grandma, I have to get home to Rick. It's after four, and we have studying to do still. Plus, I have to cook supper. I'll come back tomorrow, okay?"

"Yes, Lizzy dear, I'll be here waiting!" They said their good-byes and Liz drove off.

On the drive home Liz thought about Khafa and how she suffered in the jail cell. She thought about the betrayal from her very own Queen, the Queen whose destiny she helped nurture. How could she do such a thing? Liz thought of the present world and all of the betrayals and murders. The new world was no different than the old world. The new world was sugarcoated and nothing more, thought Liz.

Rick had arrived at six that night to find a beautifully set up dinner table by Liz who cooked up a few rib eyed steaks, some mashed potatoes and green salad. Rick was happy with the decor of candles and fresh cut flowers Liz took from her parents' yard. Graduation was a month away, both Rick and Liz were ready for their final exams. After this, there was no telling where their degrees might take them. The museum was a great place to start for the experience, but they both dreamed of going to Egypt one day where they could find the dream job they had been studying for all their lives.

The High Priestess

Liz was becoming quite the cook. Rick sat down at the table to enjoy his meal with his beloved. "Liz, how was your day honey?" Rick asked as he poured two modest glasses of red wine.

"It was great. I stopped over at Grandma's and stayed a couple of hours," she replied as she cleaned the counter. She made her way to the table and kissed Rick on his forehead.

Rick grabbed her hand and kissed it gently. "This meal is awesome. You're quite the chef now!" Rick said. Liz smiled and sat down to join him. "So, let's toast to a happy graduation and fruitful career, shall we?!" said Rick raising his glass. Liz followed naturally. Rick had a strange glow about him that evening.

Liz thought he seemed odd. "You keep staring at me? What is it?"

Rick smiled broader than ever and finally said, "I'm in training as of Monday." Rick paused to let the guessing game linger a little.

"Training for?" asked Liz.

"Well, the manager is relocating to another city due to family issues, and there isn't anyone to fill the position or rather someone who is up for it. So they approached me, being a rookie and all!"

Liz jumped up in excitement and hugged Rick and yelled, "*Whoooohooo*! You know what this means? A bigger pay check and benefits too!"

"Liz, you and I both know what this means. It also means travelling to and from Egypt. I'll be working with the finest in Cairo and assisting in the archaeology aspect as well!" he added.

"Well, isn't this what you've always dreamed of? I mean, this is all you've worked for, and to catch a lucky break this way...is like the universe is making it happen for you!"

Rick reflected deeply on her words and then said, "Liz, you and I will be apart, does this bother you?"

"Oh no, Honey, please let's not do this. We both knew what these careers held, and besides I'll make my way there eventually. It's what I'm working for," she replied with a forced grin. She hadn't a clue where she would be headed in the near future, and working at the computer shop with her mom and dad was fine for the moment.

That night Rick and Liz celebrated Rick's promotion with a dance fest with slow music in each other's arms. When they went to bed that night, neither one of them could sleep. Tossing and turning, they both avoided conversation for the fear of bringing up the subject again.

The next morning, Rick realized that something had to be done; he couldn't let Liz stay behind this way. He must give her a fair opportunity. Being a manager also meant that he was able to hire and fire those on his team. He hadn't told Liz what he was up to; he wanted to make it a surprise.

When Rick went in to work that evening after school, he was told he couldn't hire anyone new yet. He would have to hold off for the moment. He must spend six months in Cairo working with a team, which was already in place. Upper management had decided this prior to his promotion. This broke Rick's heart, but it would only be a short time before he could add Liz to his team.

Liz knew this was a big step for Rick. Going to Cairo was important for Rick. He would work beside those who had far more experience and knowledge than he did.

Liz and Rick graduated that year with honors. A reception was in place for them at the Hawanns and their friends and relatives attended.

Rick's salary would now be doubled, in addition his stay in Cairo would be free. Not much money was needed for Rick in Cairo, so he planned to forward his weekly checks to Liz's account. He wanted Liz to have everything she desired while maintaining the bills on their apartment. She deserved the very best and perhaps his guilt about leaving her behind played a major role.

Liz was happy even if it meant being without Rick. She would have her parents and Grandma close by and she could work longer hours. Liz also decided it was time to send her resumes to other museums as an entry level candidate. Still, it was lonely without Rick. She spent many nights falling asleep to old black and white movies and television shows. She was especially fond of old "Lassie" reruns.

Rick would often video chat with her for hours discussing his finds, excavation sites, and all the horrible food that was served to him and his team. The people in the region were often very welcoming and willing to work for a few dollars a day. Of course, Egyptian authorities were always lurking but helpful. Without the authorities help and consent, their dreams and projects would never get off the ground. Liz was starting to dream about being in Egypt. Her soul yearned for the land of her ancestors. She remembered when she was twelve and visited Egypt because of Grandma's illness. Thinking about Grandma made, Liz decided to head to her parents' home for a weekly visit.

Chapter 9

"The Show Must Go On"

Grandma as always was glad to see Liz. Her parents had been gardening that day which gave Liz time to pop in the back house to hear more of the story. Liz was somewhat thinner now and Grandma wouldn't have it. "Eat this and no fussing. You look thin lately, I know you're missing Rick but he'll be home in a month's time," Grandma said using the force feeding method she mastered throughout the years.

Liz wasn't worried about Rick's departure or arrival, what was really weighing her down, was the fact that none of the local museums had called her back or showed an interest in her candidacy. It was gut wrenching. At least she'd have Rick back home in less than 30 days.

Liz ate in a hurry. Grandma watched her every bite, blackmailing her all too well, "If you don't finish that whole dish of beef stew, I am not telling the story!" she chuckled.

Liz let her bask in her happiness knowing better than to argue with Grandma. Liz prepared some tea and placed some tea cookies on the side of the tea saucers and they both sat down. Grandma sat in her recliner leaving Liz the whole couch and placed a blanket on her legs and feet.

"Ready!" Liz said. She sat what was left of her beef stew on the counter without a care in the world and stared at Grandma in anticipation.

"Khafa," Grandma began, "had warned the Queen of the King's doings that day and the Queen was once again drowning in her own sorrows, in a depressive state, like the victim of brutality. Aketu had never known brutality at its best, she was indeed spoiled in her life and extremely lucky when it came to fame, fortune and status, but real love...was to never find its way to her no matter how hard she tried with her King. She carefully mastered the plan of getting Khafa confined to a jail cell for five days straight. Khafa would never forget this betrayal by the Queen she loved and cared for. Khafa thought that reinventing herself was the best way to go."

"It wasn't without fear or ambition to her projects she would make the change, her plan was to simply stay two steps ahead instead of being caught up with the dynasty and its incompetency to follow through with anything. Obelisks and monuments to worship the gods were never finished. Projects around the Kingdom always ground to a halt and Khafa had trouble understanding why, yet didn't dare ask when council meetings had become sit-ins for entertainment instead of taking business head on.

It seemed like it was meant to be this way, or rather someone was stalling Egypt's progressive state. Khafa was weary and lacking trust more than ever to all those who filled the service, especially the council members, the people who had been a thorn in her side from the very beginning. She had it in for them, and the King and Queen either played the fools or were just terrible at handling their affairs. They were openly trusting and this was to be their downfall. The members weren't stupid; they saw this flaw in their rulers who lead them down a path toward inexperienced heirs.

The rulers thought they had been doing wonderfully by tackling Mother Nature's fury shown in the annual droughts. They hadn't done enough and the birth of their prince still amounted to nothing despite their efforts to please the country. They weren't visionaries like Khafa. This bothered her dearly when she often guided the Queen on how she should proceed. Then the King came to dismantle her doings and good deeds with the blink of an eye and the Queen accepted this foolishly as a display of her being submissive and obeying partner. Perhaps it was to get back at Khafa for warning the Queen of his habitual behavior.

The tattling never sat well with the King and his little jabs and stings tore to the very core of Khafa's every move. Spiteful and despicable he was, like a child no older than the spoiled Prince he so gracefully contributed in seeding the yolk three years prior. The Prince was rambunctious and out of line, but this was due to the fact that Khafa had been dismissed from the duty of raising the Prince and inexperienced care givers had stepped in to damage any good she had ever taught him from birth. It was unfortunate, but what was more disturbing was when the Prince fell ill for days, Khafa and her priestesses were called to perform their rituals in the Prince's chambers. The Queen approached Khafa and coaxed her to a corner for a private discussion.

The King hadn't budged from the Prince's bed side in two days. It was the first time Khafa would ever see the King in this state and it was heartbreaking. The Prince lay motionless in his bed, struck with high fever, nightmares and hallucinations that cast a dark cloud over his tiny body.

The Queen cried and begged at Khafa's feet, "Please help us!" Khafa encouraged the Queen to stand and stared into her eyes with concern.

She gazed at the scene before her, taking in every detail. She sighed deeply. "I will do all I can," she offered. She administered medicine, gave him plenty of fluids, even wine and performed prayers by his side for a day and a night with her crew. Still, the Prince hadn't responded to any of it.

The King hadn't any words to spew, with anguish and resentment in his heart, he never once looked Khafa's way or acknowledged her presence. He was uninviting and unreceptive to her rituals and incantations. Khafa was unmoved by his silly attitude. Instead, she shrugged it off and focused on the well-being of the Prince. Khafa was able to compartmentalize her feelings for the King, while a dying boy needed her help more than ever. This is what made her feel human again, wanted and needed. The Prince began to move a little more after three days. He began to speak and open his eyes for longer periods of time and he was slowly making progress.

One morning, the helpers ran at the request of the King to fetch Khafa and summon her back to view the Prince's rehabilitation first hand. Khafa ran from the compound of the priestesses and priests with smiles upon her lips and sheer happiness in her very soul in the hopes of seeing the Queen in better spirits. The Prince was sitting up and had never looked better. His cheeks were once again rosy, he smiled from ear to ear. The Queen ran to Khafa and hugged her tightly. Khafa laughed in amazement and spoke as she approached the Prince's bed side.

"You are well my Prince, but you need a little more rest before you walk, understand?"

The King was ecstatic and he approached Khafa and spoke to her before the Queen, the chamber maids and the help. "I have much to be thankful for now that you have saved the heir of Egypt. We are grateful on this day. Whatever you desire shall be yours!" The Queen nodded in approval. Khafa thought it was all a dream and no credence was to be given to the King and his empty promises. She said, "My King, I require very little for the time being, maybe one day I can take you up on your offer. For now, all that is dear to Egypt lies in this bed, therefore a celebration is in order!" Khafa thought that being humble before all would give her much credibility and that she'd be remembered as the "humble hero" rather than a snake in the pit waiting to bite back at the first sign of weakness.

The King spoke, "Very well, my high priestess. We will have a celebration in your name and the Prince will be glorified by your side."

The Queen told the help, "Run along now, see it done, we celebrate tomorrow and I want all of Egypt here!" Khafa smiled at the Prince and the Prince requested her hand to hold.

It was at that moment that the King and Queen spoke almost in unison before Khafa. "Perhaps we have been too harsh on you, we will require your full attention where the Prince is concerned. You may have your duty back as caregiver, effective immediately!" Once again the Queen smiled and nodded in approval adding, "We realize there is no better than you, our Prince loves you dearly. It would be a mistake not to have you tend to him." Khafa smiled.

It wasn't long before the Queen had given birth again, but this time the baby was a princess. The Prince was now four years of age. The King hadn't favored the princess at all and Aketu once again fell into a deep depression because of it. The King felt like he had been punished for his sins, as Khafa and the King had resumed their relations once more prior to her birth. The game of love between Khafa and the King was merciless, passionate and so easy for the both. The Queen had no idea since they had done it secretly and were cautious. They did it in secret passageways; they did it in any secluded spot away from curious eyes and sharp tongues.

Khafa watched the movements of all council members, priests and priestesses on the compound. It was as if she had been reborn with eyesight as clear as a night hawk. She remembered the words of the council member who threatened her while she lay in a pool of blood from her wounds in a jail cell. *What did it all mean?* It sounded serious. The next days were all about rounding up her best men. The spy game was on. Secret meetings beyond the King's comprehension had been taking place in temples outside the city and even underground. Monuments were built to house these members of the secret society who practiced rituals of free masonry! A secret society brought together and compiled without the King's knowledge. Khafa would soon discover all its dirty little secrets."

"Oh my gosh, Grandma! You're not serious!" said Liz.

"Yes, very serious."

Liz was fully immersed in this particular aspect of the story, but time was running out and Liz had to leave once more. On the drive back home, Liz thought about Khafa and how she would manage such a powerful force. She would have to do all in her power to eradicate them. They were ungodly, and she was surely conspiring against the King and his realm was on their list of priorities.

With only days away from Rick arriving, Liz kept busy with work at the shop. She hadn't made it to Grandma's, for work had been busy and Liz had been really tired and longing for her bed. Rick was excited to come home, as the night before a Skype conversation turned into a sexual escapade for both. Six months had been long, but it was well worth it as Rick explained over the phone now.

"Honey, this place is jumping! The energy here, is undeniable, you'll never believe all the progress we made. The work is excellent!"

Liz smiled and Rick's voice projected a feeling of excitement and a contagious approach. "I'm truly happy for you and I can't wait to be in your arms again," replied Liz. Saying good-bye, Liz sighed and spoke to herself. "One more day, one more day!"

Waking up to sunshine the next day, Liz hurried to get to the airport to pick up Rick. His plane was landing in a half hour and she wanted to make sure she wouldn't miss him. Arriving at the gates, Rick was all smiles, tanned beyond belief and much thinner. It left Liz speechless and concerned. They ran toward one another and Liz could feel Ricks rib cage pressed up against hers and shrieked, "Honey, you're way too thin. I like the tan, but we gotta get some meat on those bones, ASAP!"

Rick laughed and shrugged her comment off casually and said, "You look beautiful as always. C'mon, let's get out of here!" On the drive back home Rick had been a chatterbox. Talking about his finds of pottery, mummies they hadn't been able to identify as of yet, the sand storms, and how he had gotten out just in time before the storm hit the sites. Home was where the heart was for Rick. He sighed in relief, threw his brief case across the room and sat on the couch and asked Liz to join him. "I have some great news," said Rick with a smile plastered on his face and Liz's ears were ready to take it all in.

"I have done so well in Egypt, that...," Rick paused and watched Liz smile from ear to ear.

"C'mon don't stall! Tell me!" Anxiety set in and Rick held her hand firmly.

"I've done so well, they assigned me my own team, and...I get to pick and choose whom I want, and Baby...you're one!"

Liz jumped up and yelled at the top of her lungs, "YES!" She hugged Rick tightly and Rick laughed hysterically at Liz dancing like a hooligan on top of the bar. The couple wined and dined each other that night. True happiness filled the apartment. Before they engaged in sex, they opened a bottle of champagne and talked for a little while.

"I'm so happy, wait 'til I break the news to Mom and Dad, oh…and Grandma!" said Liz.

Rick spoke, "Well, wait a few days. We leave in three months. The authorities want to make sure the area is closed off. Besides, we have to manipulate the work back at the museum this week, and it'll take weeks. But, the show must go on for now!"

Liz nodded in approval and Rick stared at Liz in an odd way for moments.

"Why are you staring at me?" she asked.

"We have to keep away from each other on sites. It's strictly professional and I don't want to take a chance by being caught engaging in a kiss."

Liz found this to be cold but she understood. "I can do this. We can do this." She walked away to pour another glass of champagne for herself. Her back had been turned away from Rick but when she turned around to face Rick, Rick was on bended knee.

Liz spilled her champagne all over herself in shock.

Rick said, "It will be hard because of this. Will you?" he ask with a ring in his hand. An unusual ring it was. It was ancient, a gold band with a blue stone on top.

Liz's eyes grew wide in disbelief and spoke, "OH MY GOD! Where did you get this? This must be from a dynasty of some sort, it suggests royalty!"

Rick nodded in approval. "You know it! Only the best for you, Honey."

Liz placed the ring on her finger, marveling at the hieroglyphic inscriptions. "Does anyone know you have this? How did you manage?"

"It doesn't matter how I got it. I was lucky, extremely lucky, not a word to anyone. This is our secret, never wear it while in Egypt, *capish!*" replied Rick and then he spoke again. "I have no idea what the inscription means. I've wasted countless nights researching, I could never come up with an answer."

Liz knew she had never seen writing like this before. "Oh! My! YES! The answer is yes!"

Rick took Liz in his arms. "I want to be with you forever and even if we don't have children, it doesn't matter to me. Being my wife will always be enough."

Liz cried and thanked Rick for the best present a woman with values could ever receive. Passionate love was made that night. The stars were aligned in a big dipper and the small one just below it. The starry sky was inviting and the weather was breezy but warm. Rick and Liz had a go at it for hours, not getting enough of each other. When they took a break, she said, "I want to have a long engagement, I think it's only right I start my career first."

Rick held her hand. "Whatever you wish, there's no rush, we're still young and time is on our side." Liz kissed Rick on the forehead lovingly and a session of play fighting began.

Jet-lagged Rick made his way back to work a day later. The museum insisted that their staff be well rested and ready to take on weeks of work before their second departure. Therefore, a shopping day and visits to their parents were in order. Liz was ecstatic to break the good news to all. Grandma was the happiest with the news and Justin and Catherine gave their blessings. Rick's parents Martha and Corey were also very happy, but Martha was strict on Rick doing more in his career to give Liz everything she and her future grandchildren deserved.

Liz's life was coming together nicely and she couldn't wait to get her hands dirty in the Egyptian sands. There was a month left to go. Rick's museum staff had almost finished their documented finds and displayed them proudly for the public. Liz would leave the computer shop her dad, Justin, owned. She wanted to get better acquainted with the staff, but be briefed and trained in Egypt. It was exciting for Liz, and getting up early every morning to join Rick and his team had placed purpose in her heart and a determination so strong that she promised herself she would be one of the best on this mission.

Khafa

Visiting Egypt at the age of twelve was a distant memory. Landing in Cairo made Liz shake at the knees. Rick, Liz and of course Grandma, who was well enough to travel, joined them. Grandma would visit her sister in Saqqarrah. Liz was grateful for her accompaniment on the long flight. Grandma told the story once more and Liz reflected on the plane ride as she passed through customs.

Khafa was also the keeper of the little princess Akenta, a name the Queen chose to resemble hers. The Princess was beautiful beyond comparison. She was feisty and determined and had taken her first steps within months of her birth. Khafa enjoyed the children very much in her spare time. The King was busy travelling all over Egypt.

Khafa never forgot about the freemasons who lurked in the shadows. Khafa would make it her mission to dismantle their plans one by one, since she had regained her power now along the side of the Queen. It was in the absence of the King and it was kept quiet due to the unpopularity of the high priestess. The show went on without the King present. Aketu was fond of having Khafa's full attention once more as if all had been forgiven. Yet, Khafa played her part again.

She summoned her best for a meeting. It was to be a meeting she had planned with just her closest helpers, four men and two women. As they all sat down, she said, "What is taking place under the King's nose? Will it not go unnoticed? Gather all you can before me and we will team up to disrupt their doings, thoughts and actions. Rest assured that as long as I am here the dynasty will be protected. This evil secret coven will fall apart!"

The helpers nodded in approval while one helper spoke for his group, "My high priestess, we seek your guidance."

"Let us do what we do best--open our eyes, be vigilant and distrusting of all, take down the enemy, by any means necessary!" Khafa said with a stern face.

The room sat in silence with eyebrows raised and chanted Khafa's name like mad men. Khafa smiled her wicked smile as the helpers were discharged and ready for the task. Some of the most knowledgeable

helpers sat beside her and stood all around her. The Queen was to be
made aware of this secret coven in due time. The King would be spared
the details for the time being as well. For Khafa and Aketu had far more
power and influence over the King and Kingdom than any other. The
Queen was wicked herself, but with the help of Khafa, things would be
put into motion faster than the King could bat an eye. Days later, careful
manipulation of words and Khafa's ideology were put to the test before
the Queen.

"My Queen, welcome!" said Khafa as she showed the Queen to a
chair in her private quarters. The Queen sat and spoke, "You wished to
see me today?"

Khafa answered, "I always wish to see you." She approached the
Queen from behind and removed her crown carefully, combing out the
dreaded knots in her black wig.

"I love it when you comb my hair, the help doesn't nearly do it
justice" said the Queen.

"That's because the help isn't me," replied Khafa so confidently with
a gleam in her eye and smirk on her lips.

The Queen chuckled and spoke, "No one is like you Khafa, I would
have to agree with your statement!"

They both smiled and Khafa went for the kill. Sitting down right
beside the Queen who stared deeply into her eyes to get a feel of her
emotions, which seemed to be in check on this day. "My Queen, how
much do you love Egypt?" Khafa asked.

"Why I love her more than life itself. Why do you ask?"

Khafa sighed and the Queen spoke again. "You are troubled? Why?"

"My Queen, you put your family's lives in my trust every day. I have
served this dynasty and the prior dynasty before, for years now, how
much do you value my words?" asked Khafa.

The Queen sighed and looked on Khafa in confusion.

Khafa said, "If you were to trust me with all this, it only means you
have deep love and affection for me."

Khafa

"My priestess, of course! I would look on no other for your accurate judgement and loyal service. You are my sister in this life and in the next!"

Khafa somehow didn't believed her words to the fullest. *Who would imprison her own sister for days?* she thought. As she asked herself this, Khafa played the fool and hugged the Queen. "My Queen, you will always be my sister. I thank you for all you have done." Khafa shed a tear to make it look even more believable.

"Stop your crying, and tell me what's really bothering you." The Queen wiped the tear from her eye. Khafa stood up and walked over to the open terrace and the Queen followed.

Khafa sighed while looking up at the night time sky and spoke, "What I'm going to tell you, is very disturbing. But it is also hard for me."

"Please do, I will listen."

Khafa reached out and held the Queen by her hands. "There is a secret coven who conspires against the King." Khafa paused.

"It's not uncommon my priestess, we have had our share in the past."

"No, it is bigger than you know, beyond what you could imagine, and its taking place right before our very eyes." replied Khafa.

The Queen's eyes grew wider at the implication. "Where?"

"All around the city, below us and right beside us."

The Queen sighed and folded her arms across her chest. She began pacing back and forth for minutes without words.

"I will provide you with proof if you come with me tonight."

"I believe you my priestess, but I must see this for myself."

Khafa nodded in approval and the Queen now paced harder back and forth in shock. "My Queen, please, I meant not to hurt you this way, but you must know."

The Queen grew angry, faced Khafa and spoke with anguish. "If it's the last thing I do, I will bring down these cockroaches who seek our destruction. I will squish them like beetles beneath my feet, and you, you will see it through. Now let's go!" The Queen gathered her men to guide her and Khafa to an underground tunnel not so far from the Kingdom.

Khafa cautioned, "My Queen, you must have silent footsteps, move fast and do not make yourself seen. Understood?"

Khafa and Aketu moved across the plain quietly without fire torches; the moonlight sky guided them to a hole in the ground. The hole was covered in palm leaves and when Khafa removed them and the hole was visible the Queen sighed and stared at Khafa in fright.

"Come, now remember what I told you. Stay silent and just watch!" said Khafa. The Queen nodded that she understood. Khafa had strategically planned this trip out. Having the Queen's blessings was more than she could ever dream of. All was in place now.

Moving below the sand into the cave took them all of 20 minutes. Lights that shone the pathway made it easy. Once at the bottom, Khafa went first and she placed her hand on the Queen's arm. She coaxed the Queen with a hand gesture and the Queen followed Khafa closely. Entering a well-lit grand cave before them, men sat on the floor beside columns with inscriptions that Khafa nor the Queen had ever seen before.

Guards roamed the cavern, so Khafa and the Queen hid behind deep-rooted walls. Khafa's helpers and herself had been here before but she hadn't managed to retrieve any information on her last visit. Tonight would be a special one for the Queen's ears. Hundreds of men sat, waiting to be inducted to their realm of evil. They must have been paid a handsome wage into be a part of this society. Then the ceremony had began.

The speaker said to the men, "Enter thy brotherhood and forever it shall remain, drink the blood of the cattle, for your undying servitude and loyalty shall never die amongst us." Hearing this, the Queen's anger doubled and Khafa cautioned her not to move. Once the ceremony was over, the leader addressed his soldiers. "We will bring this Dynasty down, preparations are under way, anyone who stands beside them shall fall beside them. We will eliminate all obstacles in our path, and the reign of Egypt will fall to more able hands." The men chanted in sync and their voices travelled throughout the cavern, "In our brothers we trust."

Khafa had no words and now the Queen had seen enough. Making their way out slowly and undetected, the Queen was furious with her face flushed and red. As soon as they exited the cave, Khafa said, "I am sorry my Queen, but now we must act!"

"And act we will. Meet me in my chambers, we have much to plan!" said the Queen who coaxed the guards to bring her horse while Khafa stayed behind.

Chapter 10

"Slaughter Fest"

Khafa knew this would be no easy task as she made her way to the Queen's chambers that late night. The Queen paced the chambers frantically and made sure no one saw Khafa enter.

"Do what it is in your power to do Khafa. I leave this in your hands entirely," the desperate Aketu said.

"My Queen, I thank you for your blessings, but I will need resources and strong men to execute this terrible disease we have encountered. The King will not be so receptive since he has strong ties to many of these men. Some were even made to be his lovers."

"Khafa, I know my King and you are still lovers, and I have come to accept it. You need to persuade him in any way you can."

Khafa dropped her gaze and said, "He doesn't acknowledge me anymore, my Queen. I am washed out like the shores of the Nile now." She bent her head and looked to the ground in shame.

"You must try harder to convince him. Only you have the power to persuade him. Fix the doctrines of currency and take all the money you need. I'll allow you this much, fetch men wherever you can, purchase weaponry, animals. Do what you must and I will do my part."

"Will you lead Egypt into a war?" asked Khafa.

"It is one of the thirteen essential rules a Pharaoh must live up to in his years of reign!"

"With all due respect, my Queen, our King has barely lived up to seven of those doctrines."

The Queen smiled. "Indeed he hasn't, and so now is our time to push him toward it. We are the powerful women of Egypt. I refuse to go down under the ruling of Egypt's new rebels."

Khafa was reborn and was loving every minute of her newly restored powers. The Queen suggested that the King move quickly, but how was he supposed to agree to this all at once? Khafa knew that in the council meetings the members, who were also the members who conspired against the Dynasty, would have a lot of influence on the King's sound decision making. Khafa had been dealt the same cards she played years earlier, but now the games had to be played more carefully. There would be an infinite amount of strange things to come.

The Queen was coming to her senses with age, she had been somewhat more mature, more cunning and aware. Letting Khafa guide her was the best thing she could have done. The Queen was awakening and had become far more intelligent than the King had ever been. Khafa thought she should let the men "be", "Don't argue, just nod yes" and play the fool when things are bad. Pretend the King is always right, feed him well, compliment him and when on your own, do what you like but also, be submissive, not stupid.

The Queen had adopted these methods during the course of her marriage and it would prove to be fruitful in every way. These were Khafa's methods as well, but Khafa always pushed her own agenda behind the scenes. Khafa also refused to be outsmarted in any way shape or form.

She spoke to herself, "I will never fall, I shall only rise." Khafa knew how to play the King, she knew the King would often be moody and demanding. To play on his every emotion was key. She would offer him goods he couldn't refuse—exotic treasures, all the men and women he could possibly enjoy. These were the first steps. With the backup of the Queen now, the King would have no choice but to be open to her and be submissive to her.

Then the young Prince fell ill again! For two days and two nights, he had high fever. Nothing Khafa and her priestesses could do would save the young Prince. On the third day, the young Prince died.

Egypt was once again at the mercy of another stall. The King was livid walking around the palace in anger and shouting, "What am I to do with a princess only!" His shouts were unreasonable for his Queen was young and able to produce more children. The Queen locked herself in her chambers for days and the city was in mourning as the young Prince had been mummified for his peaceful journey of "westing." Khafa was distraught, she had done all she could and the Queen knew this wasn't her fault. The King embraced her even more on their secret sexual escapades. He was a broken soul, and once again he talked about his punishment by the gods who hadn't favored his union with Khafa.

Khafa was exhausted to live in this fashion and she longed for real love. She wanted a love where it wasn't necessary to hide. She shifted her gears and went to see the Queen after a week had passed and the reality of the prince's death begun to really sink in.

Someone knocked on the Queen's door and the helper came to attend Khafa on the other side.

"The Queen wishes to speak with no one at this time," said the helper as she tried to shut the door.

Khafa stopped her and spoke, "The Queen will speak to me, I come for an urgent matter. Move out of my way!" Making her way through the chamber, she saw the Queen on her chair overlooking the Nile. Her face showed anguish in her soul. She had been a wreck, she looked like she hadn't slept in days, her hair was undone, her wardrobe the same as the one she buried her child in days ago, she was a complete and utter depressed mess.

Khafa came closer and put a hand on the Queen's shoulder, "You must get cleaned up to face the people of the city and most of all...we have tremendous work ahead of us. It is time."

"You are the voice of reason. What would I do without you?" She slowly got up and wiped the tears from her cheeks.

Khafa told her, "You will bathe, and come stroll with me on the compound. We have much to discuss."

"I have so much gratitude for all you've done. The King is absent on a hunting trip for weeks. So, we will make our moves, today, tonight, however we see fit!"

Khafa smiled and exited the chambers for her compound. Two hours later, the Queen arrived at the compound in better spirits. Khafa was happy to see Aketu smile once more. Hours had gone by where Khafa and the Queen plotted all they could. They would have to move at a decent pace. Khafa didn't want anyone to catch on for the sake of being unaccountable of any crimes and schemes.

Khafa moved across the desert plains to gather all the venom from cobra snakes she could. Bottles of venom were being filled up by her and her helpers. A carriage full pulled by oxen was lead to the dungeons of the priests. The bottles were safely tucked away in a corner under Khafa's watchful eye. She made all her helpers pledge silence or beheading would bestow them. The first plan had gone off without a hitch. She sent more helpers to investigate at a distance the doings of the secret society, as the Queen also prepared some schemes of her own.

That night two important members of the secret society who posed as council members met their fates when they were slayed in their beds while sleeping. Strong men had buried the bodies out in the desert miles away from the palace unseen.

Morning came swiftly in the city. The Queen had been yelling for over an hour and pacing the palace in anger. She ordered all chambers, compounds and housing facilities to be searched for the gold coins and jewelry missing from her vault. Khafa paid no mind to her as she knew the Queen's plans were to hold a council meeting as soon as the searches were almost done. That left five chambers to be searched in the member's absence. Khafa would be on her compound practicing her usual daily rituals with plenty of witnesses to vouch for her. The meeting was in place now as the helpers brought in one last member to fill his seat and the Queen sat there playing her part.

The council member asked, "My Queen, may we ask what the chaos is about in the palace this morning? Why are the guards searching all?" The others nodded in agreement

"Gentleman, it appears there is a thief in our palace, my jewelry and gold coins are missing so please be seated!"

The members looked at each other in shock and disbelief.

The Queen continued, "I need your help this morning to catch our culprit. With your extensive insight and experience we will bring whomever it was to justice, do you concur?"

One of the members stood up to say, "My Queen, this is an act of rebellion. We will aid in your mission." As he spoke, two guards walked in and whispered in the Queen's ear. The Queen raised an eyebrow and looked on the members with evil eyes. The members realized trouble was brewing because the number of guards had now doubled in the chambers. A member stood up and said, "My Queen, what is going on here?"

"You say you shall aid in my mission, you say you will protect the realm, you say many foolish things and yet you stand here before me and LIE!"

The members had now been confused and the guards stepped in to hold the members' arms firmly behind them. One member said, "We have no quarrel here with you, we demand an explanation!"

"Guards! Bring me the finds from their chambers!" yelled the Queen coaxing the guards to walk in with golden trays filled with coins and jewelry as they placed them on the table for all to see. The members were shaking their heads in disbelief and disgust and the Queen spoke again. "Gentlemen, these were found by our maids, the very same maids, who clean your quarters, and wash your filthy attire. The very maids who serve you to the fullest; the maids who fuck you by night to make extra coin. And you dare ask for explanations?" The Queen paced among the members peacefully, knowing this plan was well carried out.

A council member yelled out, "NO! This is an ambush, we would never!"

The Queen interrupted his plea. "You would never what? Steal from me? You have and you are the culprits. Incarcerate them. They will be hung in three days' time!" The guards rounded up the seven men who kicked and screamed and begged for mercy, but the Queen didn't budge at the sound of their anguish. That was just the beginning.

Those seven men had been the closest to the King. On his return, he would be told of their doings and the Queen would be spared from the King's brutal wrath for her justifiable actions.

The other members watched the men being beheaded. All they could do was report to their underground movement. Khafa visited the jail cells prior to the beheadings and spoke to the very same council member who came to see her while she was incarcerated years ago. "Quite the sight if I may say so myself. Red is your color," she said as she paced before him and watched the blood drain from his mouth.

"What do you want? Leave us now!" yelled the council member while spitting up more blood.

Khafa grinned. "Why so hostile? I come in peace. Tell me why you did this and I'll see to your freedom."

The man laughed to her face. "See to my freedom? You are mad. You are a snake and you will rot in the pits of hell for this!"

"No, you will rot in the pits of hell, or rather the hole where you and your goons hold private meetings!" she replied.

The man spat in her face. Khafa wiped her face on her gown and called for the guards. "Piss on his wounds," she ordered. The cries of pain and anguish could be heard from the outside of the cell. Khafa walked away with a smile on her face and proceeded to her daily duties.

Nothing was too haunting for Khafa as her heart had been hardened over time. With an obsessive love affair, incarceration, physical abuse while captive, deception, betrayal and murder all around her, it was no wonder she carried out all plans gracefully and had shown the Queen how to manipulate pure evil for the sake of their protection.

Khafa headed to the palace to see the Queen once more that day. The Queen sat quietly alone in her chambers while the princess was being attended to by other helpers. "My Queen, I'm sorry to disturb you," said Khafa.

"Nonsense, please come sit by me."

Khafa walked over slowly and the Queen watched the activity on the compound with her arms crossed. "The other members are weary now. They'll be watching us closely so we must move even faster. Their army training is typical, yet ancient. Sit a while before your next move."

"If we move now, they won't see us coming," said Khafa.

"Yes, we use Aketa's birth celebration as a cover up," the Queen said.

Khafa smiled at the Queen, "I have created a monster within you, yes! Indeed, we proceed as you say."

The Queen said, "Get preparations under way, see to it all."

Khafa nodded and exited the chambers. She made sure word was sent throughout the kingdom and city that all were invited in two days' time to celebrate the birth of the princess. In the meantime, the helpers had gathered new information for Khafa and her most trusted came together to discuss the finds.

"My priestess, come, let's discuss privately." The helper summoned Khafa to a secluded place of the compound, whispering at all times. Khafa walked slowly and gazed upon everything in sight. They maintained a natural, poker face along with an attitude of laughter just in case someone was watching. They were strolling and having a good time when the helper spoke, "I had my very best men watch the cavern. The members have doubled since your last visit so we have a problem. Our men aren't nearly as many."

Khafa spoke calmly and smiled and laughed. "Then get more men. I don't care where they come from, who they are and what they look like. Anything else?"

"Yes, there's more...some boats are believed to make the Nile by the pale moon light in two days from now."

Khafa interrupted, "Two days! Why that's the celebration night of Aketa's birth! No, this cannot happen, they're using the celebration as a distraction to us. Seize all of today's operations, gather your men, boobie trap the whole area like they just walked into an ambush. When asked, this is what you'll reply, "The army is doing practice runs here on the Nile and all about the city. Offer your apologies and then move out. Go now and gather all the men you can. Bring them here and we will add them to the collection of the army."

The man paused, then continued, "But the King will be displeased with having to pay more soldiers. We wouldn't want to upset him."

Khafa laughed, "The King isn't here for now and when he does return we will fill him in. You need not worry about this aspect, it is my responsibility. The Queen has given me permission on all. Whatever needs to be done, we shall do."

The helper bowed, "Yes, my priestess." He left soon after.

Khafa

Khafa wondered why the boats had been coming in and what they held, so she summoned her best men to learn why the boats were treading the Nile despite being forbidden to be there. She sent them in the middle of the night. The helpers' information was not useful, so Khafa wasn't satisfied. She sent them again the next night to see if there was any good reason for them to be there. At night, Khafa's mass army moved large boulders into the shallowest waters of the Nile hours before more ships were to arrive. The boulders wouldn't been seen by night therefore it would hinder the passageway of the boats also causing some to sink. In the city, ambushes were being set up by the helpers so it all looked like it was part of the plan. The celebration was well under way by then.

Khafa opened the ceremony. Thousands of people came to celebrate. The members of the secret society took their usual place enjoying the festivities with their whores by their sides. Khafa stood beside the Queen and watched all activities, when another helper came and whispered in her ear. "My priestess, the ambushes have been set up. The boulders aren't visible to the boats coming in. Our boats hold hundreds of armed men from different lands and if they make it to shore there are ambushes set up there too. Not many will make it."

Khafa smiled and waved at the people around her. "Excellent work. See to it that none make the shores and let all unwanted visitors know they aren't welcome." She dismissed the helper to his duties. The free masons were adding more men to their collection and the plan was now revealed. All the hundreds of members who had been at the celebration were now to meet their fates.

To not look suspicious, Khafa approached the Queen later. Khafa blended in nicely at the game of mingling and she played it well. As usual, the members were distracted by the whores that night, so they looked calm and serene. To calm the members and their men, Khafa encouraged the helpers to add more barrels of wine to the festivities. Finally, the moment had arrived.

Khafa nodded and gave signal to all the helpers that now was the time to commence their "slaughter fest." The Queen sat comfortably with a look of sheer pleasure on her face as Khafa gave the order. The Queen knew it wouldn't be long now, so she gathered her best helpers and her daughter as she made her way back to the chambers.

That evening, Khafa was being escorted back to her compound away from the scene of poisoned wine and hundreds of men falling to their deaths when word came in that 20 ships or more had fallen. She also learned that those men who made the shores safely after their ship wrecked were taken into custody for questioning by the Queen. The men who Khafa's adviser managed to round up, were coming in from the north the next day. They had been summoned and ready to serve the army. All plans went smoothly and Khafa was responsible for hundreds of deaths in the Kingdom's citadel including those who sank to the sea bottom with their ships.

The Queen was ecstatic and couldn't have been more pleased with Khafa's ingenious plans. The only problem was the King! How would he react once he had arrived? "That will be my job," Khafa told the Queen. These plans were easy to conjure up, but dealing with the King was a whole different matter. How could they explain a mass killing, five beheaded council men, two additional council men missing and hundreds of new soldiers.

Khafa thought she'd have to say the truth and so she needed the support of the Queen and her many other trusted advisers. Keeping the men in custody was key for the King to see what had really happened since his departure.

Khafa counted the days 'til the King made his way back. The men in custody would not give up their masters, or whom they served. Torture tactics were not effective enough to get them to speak. The citadel hadn't been totally cleared of any remaining bodies even though the staff worked tirelessly to burn the bodies without a proper funeral. The Queen thought they didn't deserve one. The Kingdom was quiet and peaceful again but then the King arrived. Khafa hurried over to greet him and to make sure no one would see him before she did. He was anxious to see her and that afternoon he called her to his chambers.

Khafa

"Ah, my love! So good to be home once more," he said as he took Khafa in his arms and kissed her passionately. Khafa hadn't responded in the same manner instead she backed off and put her head down. The King caught on and said, "You are troubled. Why?"

Khafa sighed. "You need to come with me, I need to show you something very important. Your life depends on it."

"Very well, show me." replied the King.

Khafa led the King to the underground and explained all the past week's events in detail. The King was furious, he paced back and forth by the hole in the ground and decided he should head below. Learning of an underground recruitment facility of worship and betrayal infuriated the King. Now, the King was to fulfill his duties to Egypt like never before. Khafa was renamed keeper of the realm where she had every input on Egypt's security and progressive state. She was higher than the Queen on so many levels. The only thing separating the Queen and Khafa was the royal blood that ran in the Queen's veins. How unjust was the reality.

The King spoke to the helpers, "See this place destroyed at once." That day the secret society was eradicated. Khafa was tremendously happy and the Queen and King were pleased and safe from harm's way. The men who served the freemasons were beheaded a week later. Not one was spared for information. Khafa believed cockroaches should be exterminated once and for all, and the deaths sent a message that this Dynasty was powerful and ruthless.

Chapter 11

"Six thousand, three hundred eighty-two miles from home"

The Cairo sun was nothing like back home in Savannah, Georgia, thought Liz. Grandma Anta appreciated it wholly and Rick had already been accustomed to it. Rick's team of ten were excavating outside of Saqqarah, a couple of miles from where Grandma was staying with her sister Datekh. Grandma begged to come on the sites and lend a helping hand, but the authorities wouldn't have it. Grandma would drive the little distance with her sister to bring Liz and Rick some Fasieekh (dried salted fish), authentic Egyptian food cooked by her sister and herself. It was Liz's favorite. They also brought Kofta, a dish of spicy minced lamb that won Rick's heart over.

There were many fruits such as apricots and mango from Datehk's back yard. Liz ate all the dates as usual and left shai, a mint tea served with baklava, always on the side. What a delight it was this time around for Rick to have the love of his life next to him and some real food for a change.

"Everything foreign tastes so much better!" said Liz.

Grandma looked at Liz with a militant stare. "Why, my cooking is no good?!"

Rick and Datehk laughed hysterically at the comment to which Liz said, "C'mon Grandma, your cooking is awesome. It's just a lot more North American style."

Grandma laughed. After two weeks in Cairo, Liz was loving the work having become really, deeply immersed. Their apartment was tight but cozy; the nights were warm and the window overlooked the star lit sky. Liz leaned by the window and Rick lay in bed with the night light opened reading his daily tally of finds.

Khafa

Liz said, "Look at this sky Rick. It's so clear, there must be billions of stars out there. And look at the moon! I've never seen anything like this ever." Liz smiled a broad smile.

"I know. There's less pollution out here, Honey."

Liz wandered off a little and thought about Sticks again. She wondered if Sticks was happy or perhaps married. She had always done her ritual for Sticks. "God, Please keep Sticks safe." Liz said as shed one tear at the memory of her friend. It had been five years since dismissing Sticks years ago when Grandma was in her coma. It was the last time she saw Sticks. But she wanted Sticks to know she was engaged to be married and so happy, and that the work toward her career had paid off, finally visiting Egypt at the age of 27. That she was making her mark on the world, just like she had promised.

Rick had now become a workaholic. Liz was exhausted, and dirty, sixteen hours a day. It didn't matter because their finds were extraordinary and the team was perfect. Rick had been a little hard on Liz, just so he wouldn't show favoritism. They kept their relationship at bay on the work site.

Time was going so fast in Cairo and on their days off Liz would head over to the museum as a guest. There, she would tour the cities and enjoy a few chances to visit the beautiful Nile on boat excursions. Egypt was indeed fascinating and Liz came to fall in love with the entire country from top to bottom. Their work hours consisted of 16 to 18-hour days.

Liz had become thin again despite the delicious truckload of food Grandma Anta and her sister Datekh's new business served up near the excavation site. Grandma had to be kept quiet since the authorities didn't give them permission to sell food near the sites. Often Grandma had to flee the scene as soon as she was done serving. Liz thought it was all hilarious, but Egypt was her mother-land and it was highly unlikely she'd be incarcerated for such a useful business.

Liz spent some time alone on her excursions, Rick never had a day off as team leader and night time was strictly for sleeping. On most nights it seemed like Rick and Liz were drifting apart. Some of it was due to ambition, some to Rick's stubborn work habits and partially due to sheer exhaustion. Liz packed her bag to headed to Datekh's home for her two days off. A taxi picked up Liz and they drove off. Arriving at Datekh's home, Grandma sat under a palm tree crushing nuts while a handsome young fellow was gathering mangoes from the grove out back. Liz exited the cab in a complete trance and barely heard the driver yell, "Hey American, where's my money?"

Liz paid the driver but stood there motionless, starring at the man who gathered the mangoes. He was a god. She felt shivers run down her spine, her senses were warped and she shook at the knee until cries from nearby made her turn.

"Lizzy, come here darling. Welcome. We're happy you've made it," Grandma Anta yelled. The man looked up to see what Grandma Anta was yelling about and that's when his and Liz's eyes met. The man had no idea who she was, yet he was blown away by her beauty and intoxicated by her smile. He broke eye contact quickly and Liz turned away.

As she headed toward Grandma, she knew it was sheer lust at first sight. She was upset with herself for even having such a feeling. It made her feel like she had already betrayed Rick. Liz ran over to Grandma and kissed her on the cheek sitting beside her. She couldn't help but look the man's way from time to time. Grandma Anta noticed Liz was distracted and hadn't been working hard in her nut crushing plate.

"Your head is in the clouds. You alright Lizzy?" Grandma asked as she kept crushing more almonds.

"Yes, I am. Sorry. I'm just tired Grandma. It's been a long week," replied Liz. She glanced again to the stranger in the grove. Perfectly buffed and chiseled he was, his sleek black hair and light brown eyes were highly distracting and Liz couldn't stop staring. Every time Liz looked his way, their eyes met. Playing the staring and admiration game was fun and it made Liz remember the time when Rick and she had met in almost the same setting. She shook her head and came to her senses.

Khafa

Grandma stood up and started walking over to the house with her basket filled with crushed nuts. She said, "You know that young man there is the nephew of our cousin. He's a fine young man." Grandma Anta winked at Liz. Liz didn't answer and followed Grandma into the home. She smiled at the man just before heading inside and the man smiled back.

Liz felt anxious, she had to rush to say hello to Datekh. She made her way to the window to watch her god picking mangoes. He knew she was there, so he smiled. Liz grew embarrassed to be a peeping tom. She hid behind the shutter. Anta and Datekh witnessed the whole scene and laughed like two school girls.

Liz composed herself. "Sorry, I love the man, I mean the mangoes yes, the mangoes!" The sisters laughed even harder.

That night was a fun-filled evening with family. When Grandma Anta went to bed and left Datekh and Liz at the table, Datekh spoke of the young man.

"He lost his wife three years ago to cancer. They were just married when they found out and the cancer progressed quickly. They had nine whole months together, and then just like that she was gone."

Liz couldn't understand why she had such a sudden interest for this man's story, and why hadn't Datekh been surprised or disgusted by Liz's interest? Liz snapped out of her trance when Datekh said, "He works for the Egyptian government and has influences over the archaeology sites. He is the authority!"

Liz's eyes widened. "That is the reason you're able to sell food to us. You sneaky little ladies you both are!"

Datekh winked and smiled and didn't utter another word. Liz wanted to hear more of the man, but Datekh decided she needed to go to bed. Liz was left to take a chair outside by herself in the pale moon light watching the stars. She attempted to text Rick but then her phone rang and it was her Mom from back home. Liz and Catherine spoke for over an hour. Her Dad came on as well for about ten minutes. All was well back home. Liz hung up and tried getting hold of Rick but he wouldn't answer her texts or calls. It was so annoying as Liz tried over and over for a half hour. She strolled the mango grove and touched the fruit like the handsome man had done. The skin was soft, the mangoes ripe for the picking.

A voice from behind her said, "Beautiful aren't they?" She turned and it was the man.

Liz quickly gathered her composure and cleared her throat. "Oh gosh, you scared me. Hi I'm Liz!" She extended her hand, he wasn't receptive.

"I'm sorry, I don't shake a lady's hand. I do however kiss them gently." He began taking her hand back and kissing it.

Liz smiled. "I know who you are. You are on Rick Cott's team below Saqqarah."

"I also know you are his fiancé!" said the man.

Liz sighed while thinking the authorities knew nothing of their relationship. "I'm sorry. I can assure you that we keep it strictly professional."

"Do not worry. I'm the good guy and I will never tell your secret. Besides, there are many secrets here in Egypt," he replied

"Secrets? What secrets?" asked Liz.

"*Ahhhhh*, I thought you archeologists knew it all! Egypt! She has an enigma of such doesn't she?" replied the man.

Liz had a feeling he was hiding more and said, "Yes, mysterious she is, always has been. But Khemit tells us so much more, doesn't it?"

The man's eyes shined bright while looking at Liz as if she had been a goddess herself. "I'm sorry, I haven't properly introduced myself. I'm Hakim Abeth!"

Liz smiled and her nerves we starting to calm. Hakim was ever so receptive to her ways. Liz asked Hakim what he thought of the work being done at the major sites and Hakim answered. "I think it's phenomenal. America has done well here. My studies were completed in Europe and our system is different, but just as nice."

"You're also an archeologist?"

Hakim nodded and smiled. "You cannot be an Egyptian authority without being an Egyptologist or archeologist. I married late in my life because my career came first. When I finally married, I soon after lost my wife to cancer." Hakim put his head down.

"I'm sorry for your loss. I guess you've been at this career for a while now."

Hakim replied, "Yes, fifteen years now. I just turned 40 in April."

When Hakim said April, Liz automatically thought of Sticks, whose real name was April.

"It doesn't matter now, she's "westing" beautifully and life does go on even for you archeologists," said Hakim.

Liz was confused by the comment and said, "I'm sorry, what do you mean?"

Hakim smiled. "What you don't know?"

Liz shook her head while afraid of the next sentence to come out of his mouth. Hakim continued, "Your team has been cut from funding and you'll depart in four days from now. You'll return for the next cycle in six months. I'm sorry, I thought you knew!"

Liz's face flushed red and her heart was shattered in a million pieces. Why hadn't Rick told her and why was he so anxious to get rid of her for the next two days? Liz just had to go back to the apartment and find out why that very same night. She said to Hakim, "I'm sorry, I had no clue. I must get home tonight. It was nice meeting you," she said before she ran to the home. She gathered her belongings and left a note on the table for Grandma Anta and her sister. Hakim tried to stop her and he offered a ride since no cabs had been operating in that part of town at night. Liz accepted and off they went. The ride was quiet as Liz was confused by everything that had just happened.

Hakim said, "I'm sorry Liz, maybe there is a way for you to stay."

Liz looked in Hakim's eyes and they revealed a wanting for her flesh and touch. She froze at the thought of being in his arms and taking in that sexy musky cologne he had been wearing. Her thoughts diverted her feelings for a moment and she regained her courage and focus. "Hakim, you are wonderful. This is my stop. Thank you so much."

He smiled and waved good-bye as Liz ran up the staircase to the door on top. She swung it wide while yelling at the top her lungs, "Rick, what the hell is going on? Why couldn't you tell me about the funding being cut?" She turned the corner to her bedroom door and the light was on. The music was louder than ever and laughter from a woman could be heard. Liz's eyes widened as she opened the door to find Rick and a blonde bimbo with a huge rack in their bed having sex!

Rick sprung up and yelled "Liz! Oh my gosh, what are you doing here?!" The woman gathered all the blankets to cover herself.

Liz ran out in tears and Rick ran after her leaving the woman behind. "Liz wait, it's not what you think," said Rick as he ran faster to keep his pace while putting on his shoes.

Liz cried hysterically and Rick finally caught up to her and turned her around so she could listen. "It's not what you think, she's the daughter of one major authority officials. I thought I'd be extra nice to her so she could persuade her father to keep the funding and project going."

Liz shook her head in disgust and spoke in anger. "Sleeping your way to the top and selling yourself short. You took a piece of Hollywood to the east! Please, this is the most absurd lie I've ever heard," she began walking even faster.

"Please Liz hear me out"

"How long have you known?"

"Known what?"

This time she yelled even louder, "How long?"

Rick sighed and placed his hand on his hips. He looked to the floor in shame. "Four weeks."

Liz cried even harder and Rick tried to console her, but she pushed him away.

"And that's how long you've been courting that bitch in our bed! Nice going Rick, you just proved to me that you'll step over anyone's feet to get what you want including mine. But guess what, it hasn't worked. You're still leaving in four days' time!"

Rick shook his head. "We're leaving in four days' time and we'll forget about this whole mess. I never meant for this to get out of hand. I just wanted to make it all the way to the top and have a nice life for both of us."

Liz was furious but managed to find words, "I'm not coming back with you, I have other plans. Unlike you, I'll make it because I have real love for my craft. Good-bye Rick, it's over!" She walked away while Rick stood there without words. Liz cried on the path back to Saqqarah. It took her almost all night to walk, but she made it to Grandma Anta's sister's house as daylight was breaking through.

She explained all the events that took place to Grandma. Grandma Anta was not surprised since she had heard rumors about Rick and the blonde bimbo. Liz drifted off to sleep by five a.m. only to wake up six hours later. It felt good not to go back to work and to just relax with Grandma and her sister. Liz's dad called that morning which meant Liz had some explaining to do. The conclusion was that Liz would stay there with Grandma until her return in three months while Justin would empty her things from the apartment moving her back home. Liz hadn't really accepted the idea and had become accustomed to living on her own, but she knew anything was better than being stuck with Rick. They had indeed drifted apart and Liz replayed all the events in her head that morning while sipping coffee at the table. Questions kept plaguing her mind of how Rick could have moved so fast. Did he really insert his penis into that woman? Liz was in a state of confusion as denial set in, then anger, followed by pity. All the while she sat there and wondered what she had done wrong.

Liz was a basket case and never thought that the love of her young life would turn out to be such an awful man. Grandma Anta took a seat next to Liz that morning and started cleaning up Liz's favorite meal of fish.

"It's ok, Lizzy. Love hurts and this was just a trial for something better to come. Forget about Rick, he's not a real man." As Grandma said these words, Liz could see Hakim in the mango grove picking mangoes, and looking fine.

"Oh God, please don't let him come here." But, sure enough, Hakim was knocking at the door within minutes.

Grandma Anta opened the door. "*Ahhhh*, Hakim. Please, come in."

Hakim was smiling with a basket of mangoes in his hand. The basket dropped to the floor at the sight of Liz in tears.

"Hi Liz. I took you home last night. Is everything ok?"

Grandma Anta slowly left the room without being noticed leaving both of them alone. "Yes, I did. But I came back." said Liz while her voice crackled a little.

Hakim grew worried and wiped the tears from her eyes. Liz pulled away from embarrassment. "Stop, it's ok. Do you want to talk about it?" said Hakim.

Liz nodded in disapproval and Hakim pulled away. He told her, "Whatever it is, know that it's ok. We're all here for you and I'll be here all day. If you would like to help out in the mango grove, that would be fine."

Liz smiled. "Thank you Hakim. You're ever so sweet to me"

Hakim returned her smile. "It's my pleasure." Hakim walked out with his heart in his throat and shut the door behind him. He stood by the door for a minute trying to catch his breath.

Liz made her way out to the mango grove after lunch. Liz found Hakim up on a ladder trying to prune the tree on the top. She looked up at him. "How come you're not on excavation sites these days?"

Hakim came down from the ladder to face Liz. "I go there early mornings where I make a quick round before I head to my office in Cairo to report the excavations activities, fill in some paper work, stop off at the museum and then I come here to attend to my real love. It's very simple. This morning was an easy one for me, though I'm not usually here before noon."

"I love my job and I wouldn't it trade it for yours if they paid me," said Liz with conviction.

Hakim laughed, "What job? You don't have one anymore!" Liz smirked and took a rotten mango from the basket that Hakim had overlooked and gently smashed it in his face. Hakim stood there taking it and laughed harder. "You are a bad woman, but why?"

Liz laughed loudly and whispered in his ear, "That mango was rotten, you didn't do your job properly." She walked away with a big devilish grin on her face. After her day in the mango grove Liz had forgotten all about her ordeal from the night before, as if it had never really happened and it was all just a nightmare. Laughter and silly games were played. Grandma Anta and her sister had infinite smiles plastered all over their faces. It had been such a great day of labor and laughter that Hakim joined the ladies for supper.

By late evening Hakim decided he had to leave to be at work by 4 a.m. "It was a beautiful supper as always. Thank you ladies. Liz, may I speak to you in private outside, please?"

Liz nodded and showed Hakim out and shut the door behind her. "I want to thank you for a wonderful day. I haven't been this happy in a long time..."

Liz interrupted "I can't do this Hakim. Rick broke my heart and I just can't..."

"There isn't anything to do. I will wait a lifetime for you if I have to," he told her. Hakim placed his finger on her mouth to silence her next words. Liz stood there speechless. His hands were warm and inviting, big and strong, perfect fingers on gorgeous hands she thought and she closed her eyes. He looked on her with love and feeling of wanting to protect her from the worst of storms or an army of bandits and brutes. He slowly walked away and Liz entered the home only to find both Grandma Anta and her sister walking away frantically away from the door.

"You ladies aren't fast enough for the eaves-dropping game. You're busted!" said Liz and she sat down on the couch to reminisce about the moment with Hakim. It felt abnormal to Liz that she hadn't been missing Rick as much as she thought she would. Maybe Liz wasn't really all that much in love with Rick anymore and she hadn't even noticed. Whatever it was, Liz was a lady and she wasn't going to jump into anything even if Jesus Christ himself had come down from the heavens to claim her. For the time being, just being in Egypt was great. It was a turn of events for sure, one she hadn't given much thought to, but was happy regardless of the outcome now. Liz figured she had more than enough saved up to live comfortably for years after she cleaned out Rick's and her joint account as a pay back.

Perhaps it wasn't the most noble of moves but Liz felt she deserved more and so she took thousands leaving only Rick's weekly salary. Liz wasn't stranded; her family was nearby and her mom and dad were only six thousand, three hundred and eighty-two miles away from her.

Chapter 12

"Lost and found"

Liz felt a sense of urgency to get her life going again. She excluded love, but instead she made friends she enjoyed hanging around. One was Lucia Tremonti, an exchange student from Italy studying Egyptology at the University of Cairo.

Lucia wasn't into studying when she hooked up with some cool kids who just wanted to party. Liz liked Lucia because she was much like Sticks, but with a brain. Liz was hoping to escape from her problems of having no job and no fiancé.

Even after a full month of trying to figure it out, she couldn't figure out why Rick was always there. It was perhaps because he kept texting her and asking her to take him back. He said being in America away from her was lonely. She ignored him and never talked to him again after she caught him in bed with that other woman. When Lucia passed around a joint, Liz refused it even though she thought about something harder to take the edge off.

"Hey Liz, there's a rave party down in Saqqara tonight. Let's take this and we'll be good to go!" Lucia said.

Liz looked at the pills. "What are those?"

"It's speed and it'll make you feel invincible. You'll dance 'til your legs fall off!"

Liz laughed and thought it over for a minute. "I've never done drugs in my life. But, why not?!" Liz took a pill and Lucia swallowed one as well.   They laughed like silly teenagers. On their way to the rave, Liz felt like she had to move at all costs. They entered an abandoned warehouse on the outskirts of Saqqara not too far away from Grandma Anta's sisters home.

The place was on "fire" with people everywhere. Liz hurried to the dance floor and swung Lucia to her side and told her, "I've never been to a rave either. This rocks!" Liz and Lucia pulled off some pretty seductive dance moves. From a distance Liz saw a man who resembled Hakim. She kept seeing visions of him watching her and Lucia reassured her that there was no such man.

It was so liberating to Liz to finally let go, to be wild and free, able to let loose and not worry about tomorrow or worry to make class on time like she had for many years or her younger years of being bullied, her graduation, applying for museums who hadn't favored her candidacy, a betrayal from her future husband, and working her fingers to the bone in the family's computer shop. It was all so stressful. That night was her chance to let go of all of it.

While she danced, she thought of Hakim, and if he had been there, she would seductively put on a show for him, letting him know she was dancing for him only. The men flocked around her, and Liz was right, the visions she saw of Hakim haunting her, were real! Hakim was there, only because the abandoned building was standing on a graveyard of ancient artifacts and Hakim was called to supervise the warehouse until the party was over when they would start bulldozing the place down. It was indeed the last rave party the warehouse would see.

Hakim was taken by Liz's moves. She was a temptress, skillful and mind blowing. She made him rock hard, but envy and jealousy took over when some men started rubbing up against Liz. Hakim decided he'd had enough. He bolted over to stand right behind her as the men moved away Hakim began rubbing against her instead. Liz was fully into her moves. As she turned around, she wasn't shock one bit. Instead, she played the part well, put her hand around him and spoke in his ear, "I knew you were here, I was dancing for you!"

Hakim caressed her curves and asked her to step outside for a brief moment. Liz was in a state of bliss, the drug had taken its full effect and energy and sex was on her mind. "Liz, what are you doing here? This isn't your style!"

"My style? Why are you here? Aren't you a little too old for raves mister?" she replied and poked his chest with her index finger.

"Yes, I am and so are you. But I'm here on business and you're here for fun. I think I'll take you home Liz, I'm worried."

"I'm not your baby to take care of. Take me home? Please, I'm going back in," said Liz as she stepped away and headed for the door.

Hakim took her gently by the arm and swung her back to meet his face. "Don't get lost, Liz. You don't need this life style." He looked on her with love and care in his eyes.

"What do you care what I do? I'm jobless, homeless, stuck in a country I love to hate because opportunities are right at my feet, yet I can't seem to grasp at them because some fucker with 20 diplomas and 20 years below his belt is hogging it all. What do you know about what I need and want?" replied Liz in anger.

Hakim took Liz in his arms. "Be patient. I love you, Liz."

Liz stepped back and looked confused as tears filled her eyes. Her black eyeliner started to run. "Love? Who needs it?" She left Hakim to his sorrow and entered the building once more where she took center stage and danced the night away. Hakim couldn't bear being in the same place as Liz, so he ordered a replacement and headed home until the next day.

Days had passed after the rave party and Hakim still hadn't come around to tend to the mango grove. Liz remembered how foolish she must have looked in front of Hakim. The drug was enticing for Liz, she had taken to it well. It made her confident and wanted again. Even though Hakim wanted her at any cost, she refused to be with anyone.

Even Hakim though it killed her, especially since she wanted him just as badly. Liz was going to stay true to her heart no matter what. A rebound relationship was the last of samples on her list now. Liz had taken on the task of pruning the mangoes when Lucia came around one morning. Hakim was behind her but stayed hidden. Lucia sparked a joint and Liz took a toke for the very first time and almost choked up a lung from excessive coughing. Lucia laughed and Hakim laughed silently from behind a bush.

Lucia said, "So this guy, Hakim, he's really hot Liz. And he has the hots for you. So why aren't you with him?"

Liz smiled and raked the sand between her fingers and said, "You know, there are days, I just want to ravage him whole. But I guess that's ovulation doing its biological work. Then there are days I just want to love him like a mother loves her baby. To take care of him and cook him the meal of a lifetime. I don't know Lucia, I'm so messed up, I would only hurt him. Besides, I feel like such a loser without a job right now. I'm not good enough for a man like him."

Hakim took in Liz's words. It was apparent what she had been really feeling for him. He knew she loved him back and it gave him an incentive to put together his plans for the future.

"See, I knew it, you answered the question with almost the same answer. Either way, you love him," said Lucia.

Liz laughed. "I do Lucia, I really do."

Hakim decided he would make his presence known and pretend he had been out of breath from walking over. "Hello ladies," said Hakim.

Liz smiled a Mona Lisa smile and Lucia said hello.

Hakim said, "Sorry friend, may I have a word alone with Liz?" Lucia walked away.

Liz said, "I'm sorry about the other night. I was on speed and it fogged my judgement a little."

"I figured you were on something. Everyone in those raves is. So it's alright. I'm sorry too, Liz. I should have never groped up against you like that and asked you to go home. You are right, you're not my baby to care for."

"Well, I guess that settles it. We shall call it a truce!" and Liz gave her hand to be shaken not remembering that Hakim only kissed ladies' hands. Instead, Hakim pulled Liz firmly to his chest, a move so unexpected it scared Liz and she backed away. "No, I can't, I'm sorry!" She ran and left Hakim to fester in his agony.

Now, he had to try and persuade Liz that they belonged together. He would use any means possible but time was running out for Liz since her departure was less than three weeks away. Hakim came by early the next day on his day off and knocked at the door. Liz was still sleeping and Grandma Anta and her sister made a cup of coffee for Hakim while he sat there waiting. Liz woke up at eight a.m. to the sound of laughter. She peeped through the crack of the door and saw the beautiful Hakim having coffee. He was dashing and she looked a mess and said to herself, "Relentless he is!" She hurried to shower and got dressed. She heard a knock at her door. "Come in," she said.

Hakim opened the door and stood there silently.

"Morning Hakim," said Liz while trying to look annoyed by his presence.

"Morning, Liz. I thought you might like to come and check out something fascinating," replied Hakim with a twinkle in his eye.

"Oh yeah, and what might that be?"

Hakim answered, "The three Pyramids on the Giza strip."

Liz stood up and dropped her straightener.

Hakim smiled and began to leave. "We leave in five minutes."

Liz had never seen the pyramids up close or taken a tour there. This was the only place left for her to visit and it was grander than any other excursion. Hakim knew exactly what Liz needed that day and he would be the only one to provide her with the best tour possible. Hakim opened the door to his jeep for Liz and within a minute they were on the road. Liz was all smiles on the ride over and Hakim knew he had her in the palm of his hands now. Hakim's heart was racing. This was always a magical place for him. "Liz, you look beautiful this morning. In fact, you're looking better every day."

Liz smiled and held her hair away from her face as the winds blew them. "I'm happy. Thank you, Hakim." They sat quiet until they reached the pyramids. Liz's breath was completely taken from her as Hakim opened her door, that she flew out suddenly and excitement was rushing through her.

"Oh, my God! I don't believe my eyes. Seeing it from far, just doesn't do it justice." Liz hopped and skipped all around Hakim like a child and Hakim burst into laughter. She was lost in the moment that she turned and kissed Hakim on the lips unexpectedly. She let go and realized she shouldn't have kissed him. It was a sweet moment of happiness and her lips tasted like sweet, churned butter, slippery and sensual.

It was like no other kiss he had ever had before. He gave her space. They gazed in each other's eyes. Hakim saw pain there still and made no further attempt to bring her to his arms or lips.

He told her, "Well, why are we standing here? C'mon, let's go!"

Liz smiled and took Hakim by the arm and placed hers underneath his, letting him lead the way. Liz's eyes were everywhere. It was so breathtaking that Liz began to cry.

Hakim noticed and said, "Oh now c'mon. Don't."

"This is what I've worked for my entire life so far, to be here, like this, with you..."

Hakim interrupted, "I know the feeling. I've felt this long ago, and the Khemitians story behind this is just fascinating. You know the story, right Liz?"

Liz was once again lost in her moment, "Yes, stop yapping and move it mister!"

Liz and Hakim walked further into the sites, then Hakim stopped her. "There is a masquerade ball the night before you leave. It was organized by my fellow co-workers. I'd like you to be my guest."

Liz paused and took in the words of Hakim and spoke to herself, "I've never been to a ball, this would be so grand." Then she spoke out loud, "I'll think about it."

"Please do. You have all the time in the world to pick out a great costume."

Walking along the path and the monstrous pyramids, Hakim's tour guide instincts kicked in, but soon Liz grew tired of the usual stories. "So, the great Pyramid of Giza, or as some would say the Pyramid of Khufu or the Pyramid of Cheops, is the largest and oldest of all three. They border what is now El Giza."

"Yes, and the only one to remain?" Hakim asked.

"To remain intact!" Liz blurted.

Hakim winked at her. "She is also the oldest of...?"

Liz answered quick. "The oldest of the seven wonders of the ancient world."

Hakim smiled. "Come, we will move inside now."

Liz followed like a little puppy on his master's leash. All around the pyramid were tourists, photographers and some had even stopped to say hello to Hakim. They knew the man very well and his status was indeed of a high rank amongst the authorities. Moving inside, they saw a mark on the interior chamber referencing the Fourth Dynasty Pharaoh Khufu. Egyptologists believe that the pyramid was built as a tomb over a 10 to 20-year period concluding around 2560 B.C.

Liz said, "Egyptologists? Please, it's all science that covers the truth up!"

Hakim smiled at her comment knowing she had been referencing Kemithology and the work of Abd'El Hakim Awyan and Nicola Tesla's theories. "Dr. Awyan seems to be a hero to you, am I right?"

"Of course, we're descendants of the Khemitians so it comes naturally. I mean, don't get me wrong, the archeologists have done tremendous works here, but I can't escape the truth. My heart won't let me," replied Liz.

Hakim had the broadest smile. "You are one of a kind and you make my heart skip three beats." He took Liz's hand and now she was a little more receptive as he placed her hand on his chest to feel the fast paced beating.

Liz blushed and slowly pulled away. "I hear you've done great work in the little time you were on Rick Cott's team. This doesn't go unnoticed you know." Liz read the hieroglyphs on the chamber walls while avoiding Hakim's comment. "You know, many dynasties and pharaohs have been erased from scriptures, walls, and any other monuments because of shame they brought on to the land?"

Hakim knew exactly what she had been talking about but hadn't dared say anything. Instead he coaxed Liz to the grand gallery to see the relieving chambers.

Liz said, "Ah yes, these chambers were discovered by none other than Colonel Howard Vyse and J.S Perring in 1837."

"Yes, but what did they use?"

Liz paused for a second and said, "Wait, I know this one."

"Time's running out."

"Blasting powder!" she answered and then winked at Hakim.

They exited the pyramid to see the other two monuments. Hakim and Liz picked up some lunch when they got in the jeep to head out. Hakim had taken Liz to have some fine lamb kebabs and grilled vegetables not so far away from the sites. Liz and Hakim had a wonderful history-filled day and now dawn was upon them and it was time to take Liz home.

Liz loved being at site on the Giza strip. It was magical and an air of sheer energy was surely felt. All tourists, documentary filmmakers, poets, and authors sat around the site just taking in its inspiration. The pyramids were muses to many in the arts and Liz was so blessed to be amongst them all.

"Well Miss, this is your stop," said Hakim. He got out from the driver's seat to open the door for Liz, but she slipped on the foot holder and Hakim caught her. She stared into Hakim's eyes and found caring and devotion. His musky cologne gave off scents of sandal-wood and spices, even a hint of cinnamon. Scents that were hard to forget and lingered for hours.

Liz finally said, "You know, we have to stop meeting like this."

Hakim chuckled and Liz joined him. She said, "Ok, I must go now. This was a wonderful day Hakim. How can I ever repay you?"

Hakim said, "Be my date at the ball."

Liz smiled. "I said I'll think about it."

"Ok, let me know." Hakim drove off and Liz's heart was melting. She knocked her head against the door regretting asking him "How can I ever repay you?" and not kissing him when she almost fell. The attraction between them was undeniable, even as some memories of Rick came rushing through.

She sat on the chair outside the home that night and looked at the sky and when those memories came back, they had been a little vague. Her heart hadn't cried for him as much and she was slowly getting used to being single. It wasn't so bad, but then again Liz had a way of bouncing back from bad situations. It was her headstrong determination that made this side of her a tough contender and a wiser and better Liz.

Hakim didn't sleep a wink that night. He kept tossing and turning while wanting to text Liz but he would never actually press "send."

On the other side of town, Liz had trouble sleeping as well. She made her way to her computer and couldn't muster up the courage to send Hakim an email. It was frustrating to both.

The weeks had gone by fast and the mango grove was more beautiful than ever. Liz and Hakim spent their days there, working it and nourishing it as best as they could. Liz had gone shopping for a costume for the masked ball taking place the day after. Liz sighed and sat in a corner of the mall weeping like a baby. Six months had come and gone, a love was lost but another was found. It had been so quick.

Liz felt like she had only landed in Cairo days ago. Now, everything was coming to an end. Because of this, she chose the ultimate costume. Hakim was away on business for the day and wasn't able to attend the mango grove and so Liz saw to it alone. Hakim wouldn't even make it tomorrow, which meant the only time she'd have to see Hakim was at the ball that night at the Cairo Event's Center.

That night Liz took a bath in bubbles, had a glass of wine and played some soft music before getting dressed in her costume. Hakim texted Liz: "I know you're going to be the most beautiful woman here. I can't wait to see you."

Liz smiled and her heart skipped a beat. "Savor it, it will be the last night you see me for a while."

Hakim was heartbroken and hadn't found the words to reply. Hakim was not going to let her go back home to her parents. Stopping her at the airport was such a predictable move, and some lovers who had been leaving any country always expected their partners to come running through the gates to stop them. But Hakim didn't want to hurt Liz any more.

Grandma Anta and her sister helped Liz get ready for the ball. They had been more excited than Liz herself. They were such lovers it made Liz sick to her stomach, and the ladies laughed the early evening away until Liz's cab driver knocked at the door.

Liz arrived at the event center anxious, but excited. She entered the doorway as butlers held both doors open, and she looked everywhere for Hakim. It hadn't crossed her mind that the masked ball was Victorian. Liz looked around the room. Was she in the wrong party? Liz spoke to herself, "Oh, my God, I'm going to kill him. This is a Victorian Masked Ball!

Hakim and everyone in the room stared at the woman who was dressed in ancient Egyptian ceremonial clothing. Her gown was stunning and Hakim couldn't believe his eyes. His champagne glass fell out of his hands and was the only noise made while the room stayed silent. Hakim knew it was Liz, and Liz kept the mask on her face to save herself from more embarrassment. The music started again and Hakim walked over to Liz. "Liz is that you?"

Liz said, "Who else would it be, I can't believe this, it's a Victorian masked ball, you idiot!"

Hakim laughed and said, "I'm sorry, I thought I told you. I must have left that part out, but you look gorgeous!"

Liz was furious. Hakim took her hand and escorted her to the dance floor and held her tightly. Liz finally got comfortable and she took off her face mask. Hakim gasped for air. Her make-up was beautifully done, her black eyeliner thick and long adding depth to her green contacts. The gold eyeshadow and the beautiful natural black hair was reminiscent of Cleopatra's style. Hakim fell in love all over again and spoke, "I knew you'd be the most beautiful, what is this costume, who does it represent?"

"Why, I'm the High priestess, darling!"

Hakim smiled and shook his head. "Walk with me, I want to discuss some things with you." Hakim took her arm and escorted her out. Hakim was dressed as the Phantom of the Opera and he looked dashing in his tuxedo and white ghostly mask. Liz couldn't help but wrap her hand around his neck.

He stood in anticipation of what this Goddess was going to say.

"You have been the only reason I stayed in Egypt this long, you know I have to return. I'll be back. Will you wait for me?"

Hakim answered by hugging her tightly. "I told you before and I'll tell you again. I will wait a lifetime for you."

That's when Liz knew Hakim had been genuine and understanding. She, kissed him furiously in the heat of the moment. Hakim couldn't believe when Liz moaned in his ear, "Take me, take me now."

That night Hakim and Liz made love on the grass of the Cairo Event Center. It was a magical night. Hakim was a god in his lovemaking skills. Liz couldn't get enough of the pure gentleman who brought out the animal in Liz.

Hakim told her, "Well, I guess that's it for the party."

Liz laughed and answered, "Thank you, Hakim, for everything. For being there for me when I needed someone."

Hakim kissed Liz's forehead. "It's your last night here, so, I have a great idea." He led Liz through the parking lot to his Jeep and opened to the door for her. "Your chariot awaits. Please be seated." Hakim drove to Saqqara to Grandma Anta's home.

"But, I wasn't ready to come home," Liz told him.

Hakim smiled and got out and opened the door for Liz. "This mango grove is what brought us together, and this mango grove is what brings us apart."

Liz was puzzled by the comment and Hakim clarified his thoughts. "You and I met here, it's only fair we spend the night under the mango grove together."

Liz kissed Hakim gently on the lips. "But Grandma will find us."

Hakim laughed. "Honey, from the beginning, they knew you and I belonged together."

Liz lifted an eyebrow. "Those two little sneaks."

"Come, I have blankets and pillows and an air mattress in the trunk. The weather is warm and we'll be safe and hidden from the rest of the world."

Chapter 13

"Love is where the heart is"

Saying good-bye to Hakim was painful, but it had to be done. Datekh and Grandma Anta were saying their good-byes. Hakim's heart was torn in pieces. His future with Liz was not so certain now, but Hakim knew he had a big job in the next months where Liz was concerned. Liz hadn't thought about anything else but getting back after six long months of exhaustion, a broken heart, a new found love, and so much more.

Half a year gone already and it seemed like only yesterday she set foot in beautiful Egypt, a country she came to love for many reasons. Their sixteen-hour flight wouldn't feel so exhaustive as long as she had her computer and Grandma to continue her story. Missing Hakim would be hard. Liz promised herself she'd be back in Egypt soon. Grandma Anta sat quietly beside Liz. She gave Liz dirty looks and Liz shook her head and removed her ear phones. "What? Why are you looking at me like that?"

Grandma Anta answered, "You are a fool leaving a man like that behind. Stupid, stupid, stupid!"

Liz rolled her eyes, "Grandma, I'll come back under some other recommendation from a museum so no worries. Besides, he's not going anywhere."

Grandma Anta said, "No, but you are."

Liz sighed at Grandma's reply. After 40 minutes in the air, Liz could no longer see land and reality hit her. She began crying.

Grandma Anta gave Liz some Kleenex. "I guess it's story time."

Grandma sighed and continued the story. "A deadly sickness hit Egypt that year not so long after the eradication of the secret society. The poor were always the first to go and the aristocrats had always been second in line. The royals had been locked up in their palace and refused entry to the sick. It was a cowardice act, but the King wouldn't lose another child to death if he could help it. Khafa was forbidden in helping anyone on the outside with her medicinal potions. She and her compound were also locked down for more than 60 days, but the King still found time to be with Khafa instead of his Queen.

Khafa had convinced the King that he should begin war on his neighboring countries, that it was time for Egypt to have a rise and fall, and then rise again. Egypt had no known enemies thus by far, but time would change this. Khafa would now tend to two-year-old princess Aketa while the Queen basked in her depression she hid well to the outside world.

Khafa knew the plague started to die off in the city and now it was almost a distant memory for all. The city had lost thousands and some of the armies had met the hand of death. It was like rebuilding a city from scratch, Khafa pushed her agenda of war on the King. "My love, you must see this through. War will bring you a mightier hand than most. You'll be loved and feared as their father and ruler. The city will be rebuilt, monuments of your victory will be up in no time. You'll be known as the best Pharaoh to walk Egypt's soil." Khafa poured the wine and the King answered.

"My love, we will have casualties of all ages and this terrifies me as a father."

Khafa smiled and rubbed the shoulders of the King gently. "If you are afraid, you will never accomplish anything. You cannot be remembered as a cowardly ruler. It's not time to be a mouse, you must be a warrior and lead your army into war." She opened the chamber doors and let in some exotic men and women for the King's pleasure.

The King smiled at what he saw. "You always know what my heart desires." He pushed Khafa aside and grabbed the exotic whores by their arms and swung them onto the bed. Khafa wasn't exactly excited about sharing the King with whom he pleased, but she sacrificed her feelings for the good of the future. By the time the first woman begun sharing his package, the King was in heaven and he said, "See to a council meeting tomorrow. You'll lead all war plans for us since there is no one I trust more."

Khafa smiled and nodded. She exited the chambers because hearing the powerful moans of the King broke her heart. She could only imagine how the Queen felt. Khafa headed for the Queen's chambers to deliver her the good news, but as she turned the corner two of her very best called out, "My priestess, please, wait up! We must have words."

Khafa waited as the men caught up. She said to them, "Walk and whisper. Be straight-faced and laugh sometimes."

One helper said, "The rebels are back. Those who fled the shipwrecks that night months ago have come back with hundreds more. Their worship location is unknown even though we've been tracking them for days. They do seem to move around often."

Another helper added, "That isn't all, I overheard the worst of it..." and the man paused.

Khafa asked, "What? What is worse than this?"

The man wrung his hands. "It's the Queen. She's in on it. She summoned the rebels and seeks to kill her King!"

Khafa was without words and shock came over. "*Why would the Queen want to kill her King?*" she thought. "*Why was she seeking the destruction of her dynasty?*"

She looked the man in the eye. "Find out why she is implicated, what is her purpose and most of all what her role is. Report to me as quickly as you can." The men nodded and ran to their duties.

Khafa lay in her bed all night until a knock on her door. The helpers were back. "Did anyone see you come to my quarters?"

The man whispered, "No, my priestess. We know why it's the Queen."

A second man said, "She has a lover on the inside. We believe he's the ring leader."

Khafa sighed and then laughed. "Of course, I should have seen this coming. She claims to be in a depressive state and stays closed up in her chambers all day and night."

The man raised his brow and nodded.

Khafa continued, "Have our best men search the Queen's chambers and fast. Do it tomorrow morning as our council meeting takes place. I have a feeling our Queen has many secrets." Khafa battled her demons in whether to tell her King or not. It was hard to point fingers at any royal for committing treason against their own.

There were steps to take with tons of proof to be placed before all. Khafa remembered the words of the Queen so well years ago, "I know you and the King are lovers once more, I have come to accept it." Khafa had been fooled by the Queen, it was disgusting and sneaky. Khafa laughed at the Queen's doings, she was impressed beyond belief while she also felt betrayed. Khafa needed to come up with a plan for the war. The rebels were coming and the Queen was their ring leader! The Queen had failed and sought no interest in having the seed of the King to produce more heirs. *"Love is a funny thing,"* thought Khafa.

Morning came in Egypt and the council meeting was well in place. The Queen wasn't as foolish as Khafa thought and her lover was not made a council member yet. Khafa began speaking with the members even though some had died from the plague in the earlier months.

Khafa smiled at the King. Khafa stared at the Queen that morning and noticed she had been her happy self again. Khafa thought to herself, *"Ahhhh,* what a good fuck will do!"

"Morning my King, my Queen."

The King was in good spirits, but the Queen was in another world, inattentive, and playing with her hair. These were signs of being in love and the King hadn't noticed since he cared so very little for the Queen. Khafa rolled her eyes knowing the Queen wouldn't listen to a word that morning.

Khafa spoke to the group. "Welcome members, this morning we speak of a subject that is important to the Dynasty. War!" She scanned the men's faces. "The King is a little reluctant in starting a war with our neighbors and he may be right. We haven't the man power or the resources yet. Therefore, I shift our meeting, to another matter."

The King was in shock and called Khafa to his side. "What do you think you're doing? This is not what we've discussed!"

The Queen raised an eyebrow and paid attention to Khafa's words.

Khafa told the King, "We have to wait. I've miscalculated and if we open war now, we will lose!" The King took Khafa's word for it, but looked on her with weary eyes and that meant that there would be words to be had privately. "Instead, in its place I propose the building of the pyramids to further civilization, to free ourselves from this Barbaric way we live. To have "light by night." It'd be grand, wouldn't it?"

The new council men stood up and one said, "This is phenomenal, I'd like to know more!" The other council members agreed so clearly these members were not in the secret society. Khafa stared at the Queen for a reaction who merely shrugged her shoulders.

While this meeting was taking place Khafa's helpers entered the Queen's chambers, searching high and low. By simply pushing a stone wall, they found a passageway that led to a discolored underground tunnel. They entered the tunnel and made their way into, what looked like a shrine with symbols of the secret society on the walls. After walking a few miles in the tunnels, the men found a hidden opening that led them straight to the Nile. They realized the Queen had set up shop right below her chambers, and that only she knew about this secret. Until now.

The meeting was adjourned after Khafa showed the members the blueprints of her plan. They wanted to take part in it, unlike the last members who sought her failure.

When Khafa met with the King she had calmed him down a little and things went back to normal after a little afternoon delight Khafa provided him. After exiting the King's chambers, Khafa made her way to the compound where her two helpers waited with information.

"My Priestess, come," said the helpers as they led her away. "You were right; the Queen has secrets. We found a secret passage way. It leads to miles of underground and ends at the Nile. Better still, there is a worship shrine with symbols of the secret society depicted on the walls!"

Khafa's eyes lit up as she placed her arms in back of her and kept pacing slowly. This is the entry point where the men were shipwrecked! After the ships had gone down those who survived went to the underground and stayed there for days until it was safe to leave again!

"Brilliant! I am utterly impressed!" replied Khafa and the helpers nodded in approval. "I'm not surprised, gentleman, that you've done great work. Find all you can!"

The men bowed and ran off to their duties. A series of questions were chipping away at Khafa's mind now, "Why would the Queen sacrifice all those men?" Then it made sense to Khafa. The Queen was playing along. Taking the Queen to the underground to have her see what the secret society was doing was just a game to her since she knew all along. So when Khafa found out, the Queen had to retreat quickly and killed many of her men to camouflage herself and wash her hands of any crime.

The Queen tried to make it look like it was all Khafa's doing, so again Khafa laughed to herself since she knew she had created a monster. Khafa now would round up more men to the army even though she had discussed this with the King when she mentioned they hadn't enough man power. This was a legitimate move unlike the secretive moves the Queen was planning. The Queen caught on and summoned Khafa to her chambers.

"My Queen, you called on me?" asked Khafa as she closed the chamber doors for privacy.

"Yes, I have. Sit, please. So tell me, why does Egypt need more soldiers? Don't we have enough?"

"My Queen, it is essential for the King to prepare his grounds and it would be unwise to open war without the proper equipment. Come, let me comb your hair," said Khafa. The Queen agreed and sat down as she handed Khafa a brush.

Khafa spoke, "You need not worry of the details as Egypt will be fine. And, remember the pyramids will be in your name."

The Queen said, "Well, thank you. Leave me now, I wish to sleep."

Khafa

Khafa thought to herself, "I'm sure you do," and then told the Queen, "Sweet dreams," before she exited the chambers.

***

Liz had now fallen asleep and Grandma Anta tucked her in with the airline's blanket and pillow before dozing off herself. Two hours later, a text went off when Liz woke up somewhere between Egypt and Morocco. It was Hakim. "Hope you're having a wonderful flight, I miss you already," he wrote. Liz smiled and held the phone close to her chest and heart and went back to sleep. Landing at Hilton Head International Airport some sixteen hours later, Liz was happy to see her dad Justin and mom Catherine at the gates. Grandma smiled and hugged her son.

Justin said, "Wow! Look at you, the Egyptian sun agrees with you. You look stunning!"

Liz blushed. "Thanks Dad. Now let's go, I'm famished!" Catherine reached for her daughter's hand and hugged her. Being home had its comforts but Liz was already missing Egypt and thinking of an excuse to leave again.

It was great for Liz to be back home, but the memories that awaited her back at her apartment were haunting. Liz didn't have a choice to go and gather the rest of her items. Dad had already done the bulk of the work while she was in Egypt.

The next morning, she headed out knowing Rick would probably be at work and she didn't have to cross paths with him. Arriving at the apartment, all was the same. The memories of her and Rick were vague and not as hurtful. Liz left everything in perfect order, but when she went back for another item she forgot in her old bedroom, she found a young woman still sleeping in Rick's bed. She spoke to herself "Loves me my ass!" Liz knew she had made the best decision of her life.

Hakim dug himself into some museum work involving theft. Files that were piled up from last year needed to be looked over and Rick Cotts' name was documented as suspicious. Rick was believed to be smuggling ancient artifacts overseas and selling them to the black market for ridiculous amounts of cash.

143

The authorities learned that Rick had just purchased a two story home in the suburbs of Georgia. Hakim couldn't believe his eyes. It was confidential, top secret information and he could never tell Liz. To do so could cost him his job and reputation and so he figured once Liz got back to Egypt, he would tell her in person.

Rick was not clever to be smuggling past customs. Archaeologists and Egyptologists had always been the ones to be watched the most.

Rick had purchased a huge two-story home with built in features such as a salt water heated swimming pool, a double garage, and a Lamborghini. Egypt had made him greedy and selfish.

Liz now had some time alone to hang out in her old bedroom that was still left intact. Catherine saw Liz standing at the doorway just staring and stopped to have a chat. Catherine said, "I left it as is. I figured you might appreciate it."

Liz smiled and hugged her. "Thanks mom, I do."

"I'll see you later, I have to head out for groceries."

After Catherine left, Liz opened her computer and her Skype account. Hakim had been there waiting with little smiley faces and messages like, "I'm here, I'll be waiting." Liz laughed and began her calling session. Hakim answered the call quickly.

"*Ahhhh*, you made it!" he said.

"Yes, I'm here!" she said with empty eyes.

"Everything ok? You look really tired."

"No. I slept seven hours on the plane. I miss you, Hakim." She put her head on the screen as if to be putting her head on his shoulders.

Hakim closed his eyes and imagined her there and then spoke after some long minutes, "I miss you, too." He shed a tear but wiped it off quickly before Liz could see. "What will you do in the next few days?"

Liz sighed at the question. "I guess I'll go back to the shop for now until some museum calls me."

Hakim stayed silent for a second and then answered, "It'll be ok. You'll see." He paused and said, "You know, home is where the heart is."

Liz looked at Hakim carefully and replied, "No, my love. Love is where the heart is. With you and Egypt."

Chapter 14

"West in Peace"

Grandma had settled herself once more in the house. She was tired so Liz let her be, but checked up on her often. Liz gathered her courage and went back to work only days before her 28th birthday. It was all she could do for the time being as Rick gave up calling and leaving texts. Hakim was ever so busy with the mango grove and work.

Long shifts were being worked in order to give her mom and dad, a well-deserved break. The days had turned to weeks where Grandma just wasn't herself. One afternoon Liz was granted a break by some co-workers who came to fill in for her while Justin and Catherine were away for the weekend.

At home, Liz opened the door and yelled "Grandma, it's me. I'm early." She flopped on the couch and began rubbing her sore feet. Liz made her way to the fridge to get a bottle of water. "Grandma, are you in the bathroom?" There was no answer. She waited a minute and still not a word from Grandma. She began to wonder "Maybe Grandma had gone out for milk or bread," and she got up and began walking toward her bedroom when she found Grandma laying motionless in her bed.

"Grandma, it's 3 p.m. Why are you sleeping?" Suddenly, Liz's heart sank to the bottom of her chest and she knew something was terribly wrong. She shook Grandma. "Grandma, Grandma! No, no!"

Liz began crying hysterically. Grandma was cold, so cold. "Why didn't you wait for me? Why, God why?" After a lifetime of caring, storytelling, raising Justin and looking after her, Liz felt helpless. Liz made sure to check her vital signs and breathing, but she was gone! Liz fell to the floor holding Grandma's hand and continued crying until her phone went off. It was her dad. "Dad, you have to come home."

Justin didn't say a word and hurried to get Catherine to the car for the long ride back home. Grandma Anta wanted to be buried in Egypt as her will stipulated and it had also mentioned leaving everything to Elizabeth Hawann and to Justin, her son. Liz would have thousands of dollars, in fact, a hundred thousand and Justin much more as his moneys would be from his father's shares, as well.

Grandma made her riches early in her life when they first came to America. She saved every penny, didn't drive and neither did Grandpa, and had no expensive habits like smoking or drinking. She never took vacations except for going back home to Egypt every year and she ate food she grew in her garden. She sold the home she lived in for 40 years when Grandpa passed away and made a fortune due to the market value being at an all-time high. Grandma was 86 and had lived a full life and died of natural causes that November morning. Liz was mortified as the coroners came to pick up the body. Justin and Catherine made all the arrangements. Liz told Hakim on Skype.

The next day was beautiful and mild, but Liz stayed in bed, crying, and feeling sorry for herself. Hakim called, "I'm sorry for your loss." Hakim let her know he was in the mango grove when Datekh gave him the sad news.

She told him, "Thank you, my love. There will never be anyone like her. I will never know the whole story!"

Hakim paused and then said, "What story?"

Liz sighed a long, terribly sad sigh. "I have to go, Hakim. We'll speak later. I love you."

"Sure, I understand. I'll be here for you if you need me."

Liz hadn't thought of anything but the memories that came crashing through. Grandma was more of a mother to her than her actual mother. Of course she would never hurt her mother by telling her that, but it was truth. Liz watched her mother sacrifice her career for the betterment of her family. That was enough incentive for Liz to really dig deep and get her career started. So she called up the local museums and went on a hunting trip of her own to find out why she was never called her back.

The person at the first museum answered, "Good morning, Michael C. Carlos museum. How may I direct your call?"

Liz said, "Good morning, Roger Weis, please."

"One moment please," replied the woman.

Liz got an answering machine so she left a brief message. "Hi Roger, Elizabeth Hawann here. I was wondering if you could call me back at 555-1245. I left a CV with you months ago in regards to the position in the archaeology department. Please call me back. Wishing you a blessed day."

The Michael C. Carlos museum was in Atlanta, a three-and-a-half-hour drive and even longer if she had to commute. The museums near her home were mostly those of the Civil War, and house museums. Natural history museums didn't really carry many Egyptian artifacts and history like the Carlos museum.

Arrangements were made to fly back to Egypt to bury Grandma's body on the premises of her sister's home. Grandma asked to be buried near the mango grove. Liz was happy she'd reunite with Hakim once more, even if under the worst of circumstances. Hakim and Liz had the best of reunions at the airport where Justin and Catherine met Hakim for the first time and instantly approved of him. The ride to Saqqara from Cairo seemed to be so short as Hakim and Justin, Catherine and Liz talked up a storm. Liz picked Grandma's spot and a tomb stone read, "Anta Hassan 1956-2015 W.I.P."

It felt great to be in the arms of the man she loved. Justin and Catherine got acquainted with Grandma's sister a little more when Hakim and Liz were off on their romantic adventures all over town and while working the mango grove. Justin and Catherine adored the mango grove and pitched in a little to see it progress further. Everything Liz said and did was marvelous to Hakim—the way she moved, her smile and her happiness.

Hakim approached Liz one morning. "Liz darling, we need to talk."

Liz agreed. So they began strolling on the path near the home. Hakim told her, "Liz, what I'm going to tell you must never leave your ears and be spoken to anyone."

Liz stopped walking and agreed with a nod of her head.

"Rick is an artifact smuggler and he will be arrested shortly. We've been investigating him for months and it turns out he had a connection at Customs whom he paid really well."

Liz froze and automatically thought of the ring, the ring she had carried on her person always, but had never worn. "Never wear it while in Egypt!" Rick had said. Liz reached for her purse and took the ring out. "You mean like this?"

Hakim was in shock. "Where did you get this?"

"Rick gave it to me as an engagement gift. He told me he was lucky to find it and that I should never wear it in Egypt. I had no idea!"

Hakim smiled. "It's ok, I will return it to the rightful authorities." Hakim took the ring and stashed it in his pocket.

They strolled around the premises once more and talked up a storm. Liz also spoke about living in Egypt and this made Hakim extremely happy. She kept changing her mind due to being unemployed and away from her parents. That night Liz sat on Grandma's grave not knowing Hakim was listening. She said, "Grandma, I miss everything about you. Why did you go? Who will I have tea with now? And the story, I'll never get to the end! If Datekh knows the story, give me a sign. Please Grandma!" Liz cried and went into a depression. No signs were given. Hakim was saddened by her words and waited for her to regain her composure before he walked toward her.

"Liz, it's ok."

Liz stood up and took Hakim in her arms and no other words were said. Hakim left Liz with her parents that night and promised to return in the morning. He also knew that this time Liz could not leave him again and he thought to himself "It's time!"

Datekh didn't know the full story so Liz sat at the table that early morning and cried even more. It was the saddest news that Grandma was the last to know of this story, a story that was told to her all her young life. How could this be? Grandma had always been proud of her heritage and Datekh hadn't seemed to care all that much. It also seemed that no one around Liz knew the story and they only knew the historical mysticism that attached itself to Khemitology. Was Khafa and her Dynasty all a myth? Liz grew angry for being left in the dark.

The next morning Hakim came with his jeep and honked. Liz ran over and a dashing Hakim got out of the driver's seat to open the door for Liz. "Your chariot awaits. You are coming with me!"

Liz chuckled and said, "Alright!"

Hakim smiled from ear to ear.

"Where are we going? And why do you have a smile from ear to ear?"

Hakim said, "You'll see!"

Later, they arrived in Cairo where Hakim drove up to a beautiful villa with a gate and a guard. He waved at the guard and the massive wrought iron gates opened slowly. The villa had a fountain at the main entrance with an open roof, exotic plants everywhere. Stunning flowers like lotuses and many others hugged the fountain and the sitting area that held benches for relaxation.

Liz was in a trance. "This is absolutely gorgeous. What is this palace and who does it belong to?"

Hakim smiled and replied, "Initially it belonged to my parents, but now it is mine. Do you like it?"

Liz was amazed. "I really do! You've never brought me here, to your home, to your castle!"

Hakim was now anxious to show her the rest. "Come, I have a surprise for you!" On the premises beside the courtyard was a door that led to the main street. Liz was curious and Hakim coaxed Liz to a business that had a sign hidden with tarp. When Hakim took the tarp down, Liz gasped for air. The sign read: *Hawann & Abeth School of Khemit*. Liz had no words as tears rolled down her face. She was paralyzed from head to toe and her emotions were running deep.

Hakim said, "So, what do you think? She'll be the first on the strip and business is booming here. We could charge a competitive rate and people will flock over!"

Liz couldn't find the words and she turned away. "I can't accept this..."

Hakim interrupted, "Liz, please you are without a job…you have nothing!"

"I can't," Liz answered. She waved for a cab.

Hakim ran over to stop her. "Please, Liz, don't do this!" Liz's heart was pounding with the fear of her being tangled in another relationship that could possibly fail. The cab pulled away and Hakim stood there pacing the sidewalk and pushing his hair back. Tears started rolling down his face.

Liz cried the whole cab ride back to the mango grove and plopped her body on to Grandma's grave. "Grandma! I can't live without you and I'm so afraid. You were always there for me!" Liz began sobbing and it was clear she wasn't over her Grandma's death. Justin, Catherine and Datekh weren't home that day and Liz was left to cry herself to sleep. A half hour later, she was awoken by Hakim. She woke up with dirt in her hair, but Hakim didn't care because she looked more beautiful to him than any other woman.

He helped her up and said, "You need to let go. She is not coming back."

Liz cried even harder and said, "What would you know? You want me all to yourself when all I want is her right now. I can't do this. I'm so afraid!" She began walking away.

Hakim said, "Liz, please reconsider. Stay, stay with me!"

Liz walked back and spoke in anger, "And why would I do that? So you can put me to work, and treat me like Rick treated me?"

Hakim sighed. "I'm not Rick. You need to stay because I'm the only one who knows the story!"

Liz stopped crying and put her hands on her hips. "What?"

"Khafa, the Dynasty, Queen Aketu, all of it Liz. I know the ending!"

Liz came face to face with Hakim. "You knew this whole time and you never said a word to me?" She shook her head in disgust

Hakim tilted his head and smiled. "I didn't keep it from you, we just simply never spoke of it. Then I fell in love with you and that's all I could think of."

Liz approached Hakim and stared at him, considering his words. Liz's phone rang. She hit the button and listened. "Hello Roger Weis here. I'm looking for an Elizabeth Hawann. Would that be you?"

Liz coughed and straightened out her voice. "Yes, that would be me."

"My apologies for getting back to you so late but I was out of town and your profile just came across my desk. I was wondering if you'd like to meet and discuss the position?" Roger and Hakim were both waiting for a reaction from Liz and Mr. Weis spoke "Hello, Miss Hawann, are you there?"

Liz snapped out of her trance. "I'm sorry Mr. Weis, I have everything I need right here. I will not be taking the job, but thank you." Liz hung up and ran and jumped Hakim and they both fell to the ground. Hakim laughed as Liz pinned his arms above his head and said to him, "You better make an honest woman out of me because dad ain't buying any more of this living together b.s."

Hakim looked into Liz's eyes lovingly. "There's nothing I want more." He spun Liz around and they kissed passionately until Hakim had Liz's pants and panties off.

Liz moaned and said, "Sorry Grandma."

"You ok? You can do this?" said Hakim.

"I've been wanting to do this for a while. I'm ready."

Hakim opened the door for Liz and they drove to the Saqqarah site where the old warehouse stood with a team of archeologists working around the clock. Rick Cotts was there with his team. Police officials arrived just in time to greet Mr. Abeth. They had a court order to stop digging immediately, a subpoena for Rick's arrest. As Rick was taken into custody, Liz stood there speechless and he said to her, "You did this, didn't you?"

Liz was caught off guard and defended herself, "No, you did this to yourself!"

Rick laughed as he was led away.

Hakim approached Liz and put his arm around her. "Now, this will be your site, and you will have a new task force in place as soon as the court re-opens the site. It should take about a week!"

Liz jumped on Hakim again and said, "You are a Godsend. Thank you for everything you've done."

Liz smiled and held her hand around Hakim's neck and Hakim kissed Liz's forehead. "Come now, let's get out of here. Our work is done for the day!"

Liz was happy beyond belief. The reuniting of Hakim and Liz details were discussed in private leading up to this event, Hakim wanted Liz to have everything as a gifted archaeologist and in the mysticism of Khemit. Liz had a rough start in her career and personal life, but Hakim knew Liz's dreams were those of leading a team working on sites and spreading the knowledge of Khemit. Living in the year 2015 was difficult and jobs were scarce. Hakim wanted Liz to have the same luck he had with work. There was nothing he wouldn't do for Liz. That night, Hakim showed Liz home and entered the home with Liz as Datekh, Justin and Catherine were making supper.

Datekh looked up. "*Ahhhhh* Hakim, Liz, you are just in time. Sit, we eat very soon!"

Liz smiled and told the group, "Mom, Dad, Datekh, may I have your attention please!"

Hakim stood beside Liz, holding her hand as she continued, "As you know, Hakim and I are very much in love..."

Datekh interrupted, "I knew it! If only Anta was here to see!"

Hakim laughed and Catherine and Justin joined in. Liz rolled her eyes and spoke again with a big grin, "As I was saying, I have decided to stay in Egypt. Hakim has made me a team leader at Saqqarah's new site. We will open a school of Khemit."

Hakim said, "And, if I may be so bold, I humbly ask for your daughters' hand in marriage as well."

Catherine and Datekh hugged each other firmly and Justin smiled at his little girl and said to Hakim, "You may Hakim. You are a good man. I trust you more than I ever trusted the last chameleon she was with!" The room laughed and Hakim turned to Liz on bended knee.

"Liz, there is a time and place for everything. I was afraid you'd run away again today and I would lose you forever. You and I are written in stone, well, not like a Rosetta stone, but you understand me."

Hakim was interrupted by heavy laughter and Liz found him so charming and alluring that she couldn't wait any longer.

"Yes, I do. Now get off your knees."

That evening was a marvelous feast of laughter and family fun. Hakim gave Liz a diamond ring when they took a stroll in the mango grove. "I said this grove was the place where we met, where we'd part, but I never said it was the place to reunite us forever."

Liz gripped his hand. "No, you didn't but I made that happen today. And I'm glad I did." Hakim and Liz sat on the floor of the grove and watched the sky blanketed in stars.

Hakim looked at his watch and stood up suddenly. "It's midnight already! We must go home!"

Liz chuckled, "My bed is a few feet away."

"Not anymore!"

Liz laughed and agreed they should head out. She went into the home to say goodnight and tell everyone she'd be back the next day. Instead, she found everyone sleeping on the couch by the television, Liz and Hakim gathered some blankets and covered Justin, Catherine and Datehk. That night Hakim and Liz made love for hours and Liz thought she had best of all worlds with a gorgeous Egyptian God by her side, a new career on the horizon and a palace as a home.

After heading back to Datekh's early the next morning, Liz helped her mother and father pack their bags for their departure later that afternoon. Hakim had gone to work and Liz took some time to stand with her dad by Grandma's grave.

Her Dad told Liz, "She was the best mother anyone could have. I'll come back often to visit."

Liz stood there silently while Justin's tears were falling again. Touching his mother's grave, Justin spoke again "Bye Mama. I'll be back again next year. West in peace."

Chapter 15

"The End"

Hakim and Liz said their good-byes at the airport and Liz thanked Dad for having "W.I.P." put on Grandma's tombstone.

Justin spoke, "I know she told you the story all these years and I knew you loved it. So I just let it be."

"Dad, do you know the whole story?" Liz asked.

Her Dad looked at her and frowned. "I don't. By the time I was thirteen she had begun, but I didn't care all that much about it and I refused to listen. It broke her heart, I'm so glad you took my place. If you love it, Honey, then love it and make Grandma proud!"

Liz hugged her father tightly and Catherine joined in as well Catherine said, "Come visit soon, the door is always wide open."

After leaving the airport, Hakim and Liz started planning their wedding. Liz wanted to be married in the spring when the weather was best and Hakim didn't mind at all. So the next weeks were all about work and wedding planning. Liz made herself comfortable on the new job with her team and new home.

One morning, Liz woke up to the sounds of birds chirping and the smell of mint tea. Rising from her bed, Liz followed the smell on to the court yard and there was Hakim waiting for Liz to have brunch. "Good morning. I cooked up my favorite, bacon and eggs, hash brown and pancakes!"

Liz smiled. "An All-American breakfast. Sounds really good." Liz sat down and Hakim poured the tea.

"So, you've been here for months now and the wedding is 20 days away. It's only fair that I finish off that story for you. Are you ready?" Hakim had a twinkle in his eye.

"I'm hoping you'll be as good a narrator as Grandma."

Hakim took a flower and threw it at Liz. She laughed at his antics.

"I'll do my best," he said.

"Listening to this story practically my entire life has been a long drag."

Hakim and Liz laughed like school kids and Liz felt a sense of urgency to close this chapter of her life.

"So, Grandma left off where Queen Aketu had betrayed the Dynasty. Am I right?" Hakim said.

"Yes! She was bedding the enemy and supporting the cause and she wanted to kill the King. I have an idea why but I'm waiting."

Hakim breathed in and began the ending of the story.

Khafa remained silent toward the King and in the meanwhile her helpers were watching all. Nothing was safe anymore and no one could be trusted. Khafa began to doubt everything around her 'til one day she was watching Princess Aketa and the princess repeated some conversations before Khafa without ill intent. She was still a child and had just started speaking fluently.

Aketa furrowed her eyebrows. "Khafa, why are you so quiet today, don't you want to play with me?"

Khafa sighed. "My princess, Khafa is a little tired. Let me have a rest here by the river and then we could play all you like."

"I know why you are sad. The men are coming to kill everyone and mother doesn't love father anymore. Instead, she loves the new man now!"

Khafa's ears went up and took in what the princess said. "What do you know about this new man?"

The princess answered as she played with her wooden dolls. "In two moons from now, the men will come. There are many, more than the army of Egypt and they will steal Egypt from us."

Khafa raised an eyebrow and remained calm before the princess. "Come with me, let's go back to the palace. Khafa has work to do."

Liz smiled. "Ok, you're just as good as Grandma. Carry on!" Hakim laughed and continued.

Khafa ran back to the palace and placed the princess on the helpers' shift. Then she hurried back to her compound and shut the door to her chambers. She paced back and forth to come up with a game plan. Then there was a knock at the door. It was Khafa's helpers asking to come in. The first helper said, "My priestess, we were just over by the bath houses and the King was bathing with his mistresses when a council member asked them to leave so they could have words. The council member is fully aware and warned the King about the rebels arriving."

Khafa wasn't surprised and said, "They will be here in two moons time and we haven't the men to fight this." Khafa paced the chambers again when another knock at the door startled her. She eased her helpers out the back exit before she answered the door.

The King stood there with a worried look on his face. "My King, please come in."

Khafa had been sweating and the King sat on Khafa's bed. "Egypt is in peril," the King said. "The rebels are coming back and there will be a war. I can't stop this."

"My King, I had a feeling this would happen. Be not concerned with this so much. You must be concerned with who and what brought them back."

The king looked at Khafa with confusion. "What do you mean, who and what?"

"It is your beloved who plots against you. She seeks your destruction to make her lover King the leader of the rebels."

The King stood up furiously and paced the room. "Aketu? Are you sure? How do you know?"

"Egypt's task force has been investigating this matter for days now and I've come across a secret tunnel in your Queen's chambers. It leads to a place of warship below her quarters."

"Thank you, Khafa. I can always rely on you so now we must move quickly. When I give the order, you will flee and take Aketa with you!"

Khafa's eyes starting tearing up and she said, "I will not flee my King. I cannot leave you behind."

Khafa

"You will do as I command and you will watch over Aketa and continue your life with her. See to her life, it is in your hands now!"

Khafa fell to the floor sobbing like a baby as the King left her chambers. She knew the King was going to get to the bottom of all by grace or by force. Khafa was relieved that she wasn't the one who broke the news to the King about the rebels coming. She was also relieved when he gave the Queen no credence and believed Khafa. Minutes later there was another knock at the door. Khafa composed herself and opened the door. The princess was standing there with her helpers. Screams from the Queen's chambers on the west side of the compound close to Khafa's Quarters could be heard. The King hadn't wasted a minute.

The helper said, "It's the King. He's found the secret passageway and he's killing the Queen as we speak!"

Khafa put her hands on Aketa's ears to spare her from hearing another dreadful scream coming from her mother's tongue.

"The King wants you to flee tonight where you'll be accompanied by our very best. They are preparing the carts as we speak. You'll have plenty of water, food and luxuries."

Khafa cried, "No, no, I can't leave Egypt this way. My King will die and I will die!"

The second helper offered, "Nonsense. The high priestess will never die. You will die an old lady in your bed. It is best if you'll take the western tunnels underneath the compound where peasant men will carry your load across the plains. They will wait for you on the other side, miles away from here. You'll go undetected."

Khafa said, "And where am I to go?"

"Go to the land where the King comes from and seek the help of his father. He will accommodate his only niece and make sure you are safe. The King has written a statement about it to his father." He handed her papers. "Take these documents and go!"

Khafa glanced quickly at her blueprints of the three pyramids and stashed them in a bag before she fled to the underground with her six helpers.

Soon, the princess was tired of walking the underground and a strong, young helper helped the princess onto his shoulders. The princess fell asleep after hours of walking. As they walked, Khafa replayed all the events in her lifetime while living in this palace and she cried for her King. Arriving at the exit, the helpers asked Khafa and the princess to wait a moment while they examined the exit. On the outside, oxen helpers waited to place the princess in a carriage with Khafa beside her. In front of everyone, Khafa opened up the documents from her King to his father and read them aloud:

My father, accept my seed as one of yours. Egypt is in peril and a war is coming. See to my daughter's safety and Khafa's as well. Let them have all they desire, and have my daughter claim her throne in Egypt when it is time. Khafa will look after her until her dying days. See to make our High Priestess Khafa content and she will reward you with her utmost devotion and loyalty. She has served us well, and she is dependable and trustworthy. Know that this war was brought on by my Queen who seeks my death and the destruction of all we have built together. For the Queen, there will be no mercy. For Khafa, she will be spared and will live on while I shall die at the hands of this war. Know that you have my full admiration and respect. Please see that my daughter receives the same treatment and that she never goes a day without love.

Your son and King of Egypt,

Takenrunh the First'

After she finished, Khafa cried. The letter was a true testament of how the King really felt. He was indeed a sensitive soul even though the stress had hardened his heart much like Khafa's. The King was confessing in this testament that he loved his daughter but it was an oddity. In front of all, he had displayed another nature but that was just for show.

Khafa and princess Aketa were safe, but back in Egypt everything was starting to unfold. The Queen lay dead at the hands of the King and the rebels invaded earlier than expected. The battle was underway and the leader of the rebels was seeking the death of the King by his own hand.

Khafa

Fires raged across the Kingdom and the Egyptian army was falling at an alarming rate. Citizens were slaughtered as the compound was ravaged.

The rebels were looking for Khafa and the princess, but they were nowhere to be found. They used torture on the leaders of the Egyptian army, still no one revealed where the princess and Khafa were hiding. The rebels knew better than to attack the King from the west where he held an army much bigger than the rebels. Taking over the rest of Egypt would be easier. There, the position of the King was weaker and the cities had been crippled due to their lack of resources and proper ruling. The King was no ruler and he managed to let Egypt slip through his hands easily. Soon, the King was captured.

The brutes tortured him for days. When the rebels had had enough, they killed him with a dagger through the heart! Many citizens, priests and priestesses lay dead and the Kingdom was no more. The rebels had won the battle within three days and three nights of horror-filled scenes throughout the land. Egypt was in a dark state and vulnerable. The Queen had paid with her life for treason against the King and her country.

The rebels put their best men to work on the removal of all Dynasty traces about the city. Obelisks, temple walls, chambers, and all monuments were torn down. Nothing was left. They had been wiped off the map completely. All those people who made it had remained in service of the rebels until another Dynasty would come to pass and reign Egypt once more. The rebels did not come to reign the land, but they were strictly there to eradicate the already existing dynasty.

Liz sat back and sighed at the story. Now she knew the reason no one ever found this Dynasty and why no one would ever know if they had really existed.

Liz said, "This is exactly how I knew the story would go."

"Wait...I'm not done yet! There's a little more!"

Liz adjusted herself on the chair and waited for Hakim to continue.

Khafa reached the Kingdom of Ranteh. He was the cruel King she had the displeasure of servicing before. Her stay would be hard. His mannerisms were cold but he treated the young princess fairly.

Days passed and still Khafa heard no word from Egypt. She was given a small chamber that held no comfort at all. She was being treated like the help, so she sought out her blueprints and planned to give them to King Ranteh. It was her way to obtain a better seat, or more acceptance amongst them.

Closing the door behind her and checking her surroundings, Khafa reached for her chests and opened the one where the blueprints were held. The blueprints were carefully stashed at the bottom and her clothing on top. When she removed the clothing, there was nothing underneath it but sand!

She began frantically searching for them everywhere and came up empty. Khafa cried and thought she had nothing left to give. She shook like a leaf in anger. The blueprints were all she ever had. She had committed murder for them, betrayed for them, and did all a woman could and now she knew it was all for nothing.

Khafa's dream of Egypt vanished and to make matters worse, news of Egypt came that night. The king had been murdered and his body torn into pieces and fed to raging fires. A whole Dynasty was extinct, but for one remaining survivor—princess Aketa.

Nothing more was heard of Khafa except that her blueprints were probably stolen from the secret society and used 20 years later. The plans were built and King Kufu took the credit for Khafa's late husband's genius works.

Hakim stopped narrating and Liz was puzzled. She said, "After all these years, all the anxiety, the buildup, the mystery and remaining at the edge of my seat for a good ending...this is it? It's just so upsetting. I expected more!"

Hakim smiled as Liz showed her displeasure and he told her, "Why would you think that? Khafa wasn't an angel, she upset the Kingdom, she was a terror and a brute herself. Nothing good could possibly come to people like this!"

Liz stayed quiet and watched Hakim before he continued. "What? Why are you staring at me like that?"

Liz laughed. "My dear, she may have been all those things, but you have to admit, she was shocking, beautiful and magnificent! She was clever in that she used what she had. She had the brains." Liz reached over for a kiss.

"What many don't understand about Khafa is that she was so much more than just that. She was implementing the mysticism of Khemit, the Dynasty were Khemitians maintained the secret society. Much like science today, they tried to hide the facts. And as you have claimed in the past, it's been covered up Liz. They were covered up and no one but the Khemitians and the true ones know the science of it."

Liz nodded slowly. "Makes perfect sense to me. It's a conspiracy and probably the work of the freemasons. I'm really not surprised."

Hakim nodded and dug into his breakfast and so did Liz.

Twenty days had come and gone and Liz was working tirelessly up until the day before the wedding. Liz had agreed that she would go to Datekh's home to be dressed so she would be out of Hakims sight to honor the tradition of not seeing the bride before the actual wedding day. The wedding was to take place in their villa, and Liz couldn't be happier. Also, their school of Khemit was well under way and would be ready in a few short weeks.

That April morning, their wedding day, was a beautiful one. Liz ran over before her bath to talk to Grandma at her grave.

"Hey Grandma, the day is finally here." Liz leaned over and kissed her grave as she put a lotus flower by her picture. "You know, the high priestess got what was coming to her I guess, but...I still love her with all my heart. I think if I had been in that position, I'd have done the same!"

Liz was interrupted as a deep female voice spoke behind her "Who's the high priestess?" Liz paused and opened her eyes wide but hadn't dared turned around. She was frightened and in shock and then the voice spoke again "Lizzy, it's me!" Liz shut her eyes tightly and shed tears and then stood up to face the woman and stood dead in her tracks. The woman was with a young child no older than seven years of age. Liz ran

over and hugged the woman tightly and said, "Sticks? It's really you?"
Liz held Sticks tightly and Sticks returned the hug. They both were
drowning in a cry fest as the child stood beside them smiling.

Sticks said, "It's me in the flesh! But oh! Please, call me April!"

Liz jumped up and down and laughed as they all joined in the
laughter and tears. Sticks continued, "Lizzy, this is my daughter,
Elizabeth."

Liz cried even harder and hugged the little girl and kissed her on the
cheeks. "You named her Elizabeth."

"After the only person who ever cared about me."

Liz stood there speechless and was moved by the gesture. She finally
mustered up some words. "What are you doing here? I mean look at you,
you look great, full of life, you're beautiful and your daughter is
wonderful!"

Sticks laughed. "We're here for you, the wedding. Your fiancée
found me and wanted me to come be by your side. I'm sorry, I should
have contacted you before. I wasted so many years!"

Liz sighed and Datekh came to join the women by the grave and she,
too, engaged in their reunion.

Liz said, "Nonsense! Come on, let's catch up." Liz dragged young
Elizabeth and Sticks inside the home where there they had the most
magnificent time talking up a storm. "What have you been doing?"

Sticks was her usual chipper self and said, "I married ten years ago
and just recently got divorced. I married "the big cheese" at the Doritos
plant, John Westing. It was no big deal, he was sleeping with the help
and so...here I am!"

Liz laughed. "Oh, c'mon. Is that all? I know there's more!"

Sticks smiled. "You still know me well Liz. I'm happy to be here."
Sticks hugged Liz again and began talking about her travels to India,
Tokyo, Australia, Europe and now finally Egypt. Sticks was now a lady.
She had finally settled down with a millionaire and had a daughter with
an ex-husband. Sticks was to stay in Egypt for a few months as she had
done often when she traveled the world to educate herself. Sticks had

plenty of experience as she played many men in the past with blackmail and gotten everything she ever wished for. She lived a comfortable life back in Los Angeles, but there was always one thing missing. The love she had for Liz.

"So, that makes you, my modern day High Priestess!" said Liz.

Sticks laughed and said, "I have no idea who she is, but whatever floats your boat!"

Liz and Sticks laughed hysterically while Elizabeth and Datekh strolled the premises. Sticks dressed Liz's hair and touched up her makeup. She helped her on her special day.

Liz told her, "You know, I don't have a matron of honor and I would really love it if you would be!"

Sticks froze and sighed "Oh, I don't know if I deserve that title. I haven't been there for you in ages. I can't accept that."

"No, you must! It's my fault for letting you go the last time, I was mean and I'm so sorry. I truly am!"

Sticks cried before Liz. "Oh alright! I'll do it, now stop making me cry! My makeup is running and so is yours!" The reunion was a perfect one thought Liz.

Later, Sticks thought Liz looked perfect walking the down the aisle. Liz was before Hakim. "Thank you for finding Sticks," she said. Everything that was important to Liz in the past was now returning. Hakim truly loved her beyond words and sought to make all her wishes come true using his influence and power. Remembering that Egypt did have the so called "Light by Night," Liz thought that now that the wedding was done, and with Sticks here to stay a few months, it was time to implement the mysticism in her curriculum.

Chapter 16

"Grabbing the bull by the horns"

Liz and Hakim had a wonderful time in the days that followed their wedding. They hadn't moved from Egypt, since everything Liz had ever dreamed of was right where she stood. Catherine and Justin left the country days after and Liz let her team in Saqqarah do the work while she took initiative on the school of Khemit. She would teach on Saturday and Sunday mornings 'til noon. Liz didn't mind the extra work since the school was connected to her home and the site at Saqqarah wasn't active on weekends.

Four hours of what she loved to do, two days a week, would be a breeze. Liz had begun classes only weeks later and that Saturday morning she walked in the room to find twenty-two smiling students ready to begin their day. Going down a list of students, Liz called all the names and each one stood up to introduced themselves. Only one remained seated in the back of the class and even Sticks joined the study as well. Liz made her way to the back of the class to meet a man who did not stand up. Liz took another step and screeched out loud as Allan Wellington smiled at her.

He said to her with a smile, "I knew you'd make it. So, if you please, carry on, I want to learn all about Khemit!"

Liz ran over and hugged her History teacher from back home in Georgia. He had flown thousands of miles to see her work and give her the praise she so longed for.

"I'm honored beyond words," Liz told him. Mr. Wellington smiled and winked. She returned to the front of the room. "Most of you are here because you are fascinated with the mysticism of Khemit. Most of you only know very little of it, and some of you are well into its teachings judging by your profiles."

Liz passed around information on paper from seat to seat and Mr.
Wellington smiled and whispered when she came to his seat, "You will
be marvelous. This I know."

Liz smiled, "No talking in my class."

Mr. Wellington chuckled and was reminded of a time where Liz was
repeatedly asked to be quiet in his class. Liz had been passing around a
pop quiz to learn what everyone knew so she could introduce the study at
a certain pace without scaring off the ones who knew little.

"So, if you'll please fill in the sheet, I will give you ten minutes for
these five questions and no more. They are basic as you can see and I will
read them before we begin."

To Liz's surprise, Sticks knew more than she had lead on, and Mr.
Wellington knew absolutely nothing. This made Liz smile in anticipation
of when they would begin to dig deeper, it would bring out the debates
Liz wanted in class. It was absolutely delightful to run the show thought
Liz. This was once again the work of Hakim who called on Mr.
Wellington to attend their school.

Hakim was a human computer. Now an important decision that
would also change his life for the better was in question. In 2014, the
minister of Egyptian antiquities faced a jail sentence of theft from the
great pyramid. Questions arose about him being connected to Rick Cotts,
a possible co-conspirator in the matter. Zahi Hawass had denied all
charges and was freed after an extensive investigation and the best of
lawyer's money could buy. Rick Cotts hadn't been so lucky and faced a
jail sentence for smuggling ancient artifacts. The position of Minister of
Egyptian antiquities was now awarded to Hakim.

Life was wonderful for the newly married couple. Remembering
Khafa and her life path, Liz would always drift off to the ancient world
and try to picture herself as she had once been. Nothing more was ever
heard of Khafa or the princess, except that Khafa had indeed died an old
woman in her bed, lonely and frail with no one around her. Her hands
rugged and callused from working with the help after years of living in
the lap of luxury. She was essentially reduced to being a slave in the

Kingdom of Ranteh. The princess eventually married, but never became Queen and she died in her early twenties after a hard child labor when she was bearing the seed of her cousin the Prince. It was a tragic ending for our High Priestess, thought Liz. She had grown fond of Khafa over the years and had missed Grandma's storytelling and now she knew what was to come next.

Months had passed and Liz was busy at her archeological sites excavating and making headlines with the Egyptian authorities. The Khemit school was going well, but Sticks had gone back home to Los Angeles. Liz was ill every morning for several consecutive days. When she threw up at an excavation site one morning, Liz had a feeling that one of her most feared obstacles was beginning—pregnancy! Liz ran over to their local doctor that afternoon and the doctor confirmed she was indeed carrying. And when the doctor listened closely, he told her it was twins. Liz wasn't in shock since she knew they hadn't used protection. Besides, they swore to one another they would face whatever happened. After all, that was the meaning of marriage for them.

Months had passed and Liz was having a bad pregnancy. Justin and Catherine were back in Egypt to help her. Excavation sites were off limits for pregnant archeologists or site workers since it was highly toxic to the womb. Liz was miserable with boredom, but most of all trapped by nausea, heartburn and constipation. No matter what Liz tried, these uncomfortable symptoms always lingered. Her most comforting moments were when she had to go for ultrasounds and doctors' visits, but other than that, Liz felt betrayed by her body.

When delivery day arrived, the twins were gorgeous little girls, weighing in at six pounds, eight ounces each. Liz and Hakim took their first look at them and decided on their names. "This one will be Khafa, and she will be Anita!" said Liz nta.

Hakim smiled wide. "Indeed they are, my little angels." He then cried over the beauty of these little babies. The Hawann's were ecstatic grandparents and happy to assist in any way possible. It was a joyous time for all. Over time, the girls grew up to be lovely little ladies, quick and bright.

Little Khafa was indeed feisty and clever like the High Priestess and Anta was a sweet soul, nourishing and possessing a lovely attitude. Years later, Liz gathered her girls of age ten and began telling them the story of "Khafa The High Priestess." It was just like Grandma had done for her when she was their age.

Liz had accomplished most of what she had set out to do in her lifetime. Anger, defeat, failures, hardships, obstacles, joy, love, romance, hard work and more hard work was something all humans faced throughout a lifetime. But her proudest achievement were her girls. They brought her profound happiness.

The school of Khemit was her muse and inspiration to all of her works. She had been an accomplished archeologist, a great mother and a wonderful partner to Hakim. Liz took chances with her passions and never looked back.

Chapter 17

"The Science and Mysticism of Khemit"

This chapter is dedicated to all those who have never heard of Khemit. Egyptology does not cover the mysticism or offer valid explanations at Egypt's sites, so bringing my readers insight on the teachings of world renowned Indigenous Egyptian Abd'el Hakim Awyan is important to me.

He is known as the "Keeper of the Keys" and a man I mention frequently in this story. He developed the discipline of Khemitology. His teachings offer an alternative and a higher dimensional perspective of Egypt's heritage. Ample evidence of dazzling aberrations has been discovered throughout Egypt. The evidence leads many to believe that there was a leading edge civilization left behind more than ten thousand years ago.

Man has always been skeptical, critical and judgmental, but we must remember that an open mind and the teachings of those who still walk Egypt's sands and soils are ever so important to add to our collection of what we've been taught. In my fictional story, a young Liz takes on Mr. Wellington, her teacher in history class. On the subject of Khemit, Liz later did as she pleased and educated many on the subject. Here is the curriculum Liz was teaching and where Khafa and her dynasty knew all too well, along with those who were unsuccessful in introducing it to all of Egypt at the time.

Although Abd'el Hakim Awyan originated the discipline and launched Khemitology as a whole, Khafa and her beliefs had initiated the art form with the building of the great pyramid which was once her project. The ancients and indigenous used to describe Egypt as the "black land" after it's opulent, dark alluvial soil beside the Nile. The land was nourished along its banks during its annual flooding each summer. This enhanced the rituals of the priests and priestesses who held the responsibility for an abundance of food supplied from a rich agriculture.

The sophisticated civilization left behind fascinating evidence from over 10,000 to 65,000 years ago. There is evidence of self-awareness and deep resonance with nature, enabling them to develop devices and state of the art advanced technologies that bemuse us today. The ongoing research today points out the implications and the affirmations that the Khemitians left behind for us to unearth.

The ancient Khemitians, referred to later as "Sesh", became the original forty-two tribes of Africa. They recognized their correctness to all that is, considering themselves equal in every way to, people we now refer to as Hebrews, Tibetans, Russians, Europeans and the many tribes of our black African nations. These people are descendants of the Khemitians.

They were highly advanced people who utilized 360 natural human senses, making them capable of great feats manifesting, alchemy, and trans-dimensional journeying. What does this mean? It means they hadn't a need for oral or written language, or the confines of labels. They lived in harmony and at peace with rhythms, frequencies and energy of their environment and cosmos.

All over the world ancients had built solid and unfathomable structures, employing environmental elements, combining them with the natural energy emanating for the earth's ley lines, constructing in tissues of sacred geometry demonstrating cosmology and the energetic makeup of our holographic universe. Supremely intelligent and evolved more than ever, their works speak for themselves.

A complexity of stone structures in ancient Khemit were increased and utilized energy of the ley lines, they were elaborate and included the placement of prodigious blocks of granite such as alabaster, sandstone, limestone, basalt and white calcite. Each entailed its unique energetic gear, often transported from exceedingly long distances. During the Dynastic and Ptolemaic times, many of these blocks were quarried to build temples, statues and buildings, and most often to rebuild over existing temples, many of which may have crumbled or have been destroyed in wars.

It is clear to the study and research of Khemit that much of the writings found in and around the sacred sites are often misleading and blatantly wrong! The Sphinx (Tefnut) and the Giza pyramids are far more ancient than our text books tell us. The ancient pyramids were NOT created to be tombs!

As we discretely stated in our story, Liz mentions the water tower of energy built by Nikola Tesla, the man she believed was closer to the truth than any other had been before. Khemit would offer explanations rather than a guess and here's why: All monuments, temples, and pyramids were initially built and used as energy devices for transmitting and being a recipient of natural energy and/or signals and as consciousness raising devices, or even perhaps an intergalactic communications or travelling devices.

Complex architecture, made from the natural elements of energetic rock, amalgamated the frequencies of sound and the fluctuating temperatures of running water, were all adequately working as one to generate power. The Per Neter complex (pyramid) was networked in a vigorous design of underground tunnels and shafts suggesting an even wider scope of justification and capacity.

We speculate that their technologies often used frequency, rather than machining or tools, indicative of a senior level of intelligence. Khemit research shows that the ancients possessed the knowledge and the aptness to change the consistency or molecular structure of matter itself-and therefore many of Khemits arguments and questions of construction techniques and gravity became mute!

Khemit provides a vast range of knowledge, one that could change our world today if implemented properly. Presently, Earth and its inhabitants are in grave danger from our own synthetic technologies – including evaporative nuclear power plants. Abd'els dream was to unveil the Khemitian's knowledge of free and natural energy, exactly like Nikola Tesla set out to do in 1920.

Inspired by the corruption of the world's economy based on oil, he thought, as many of us do, that it would ignite an amazing new dawn of existence and hope for all of us, but
gain, higher forces would not see a profit on their margins
if this were ever to become reality.

Chapter 18

"Forget what you've been taught, it's wide of the mark!"

In my story, Khafa had the blueprints to the fascinating "Great Pyramid" and its underground tunnels and shafts mentioned in the "Per Neter," or pyramid, chapter. It had indeed generated power and her so called "light by night" theory when it became a reality some 20 years later on the completion of its construction.

Millions believe that the urbanity design and function of the pyramids and other megalithic monuments can only insinuate that they were built by aliens or by Egyptians gods and goddesses that once walked the earth. Khemit says, "Absolutely not!" Human nature is to trademark anything we cannot comprehend as divine, supernatural, miraculous and magical. It is also in our nature to shun things that we do not grasp easily even though there is always a logical explanation backed up by science, which isn't all that logical itself on some levels.

These were the very topics and disturbances Liz faced in her life. She was somewhat of an activist and a seeker of truths and Khemit was a topic of conspiracies. According to Hakim and indigenous traditions worldwide, life on earth cycles through eternal dark and golden ages. Hakim would often exclaim: "There is nothing new under the sun!" This is implying that everything exists, and always has, in the present. Everything is in a constant state of transformation and exists in an ever spiraling, cyclical and holographic matrix. Emergence and growth of life on earth was a typical view of the Khemitians beliefs, retreat and rebirth traversing hundreds of thousands of years.

Going back to a misconception about the building of the sphinx, as I mentioned earlier, textbooks tells us they were built much earlier.

What I didn't mention was those textbooks tell us that it was built by thousands of peasants with 2.3 million blocks of granite and limestone, weighing in anywhere between 2.5 and 100 tons and over the span of 20 to 60 years. If it was to serve as a tomb for a Pharaoh so why the need for "The Valley of the Kings"? This valley is where royalty had been buried, leaders such as King Tuthmosis the first, Ramses (1 through 9), Hatesphut, Amenhotep the first and Tutankhamun.

The pyramid was said to be built around 1500 B.C and text books tell us that pyramids were no longer tombs. For example, the step pyramid in Saqqarah which did house a King at one point in time in its burial chamber and the other flat top pyramid are the only recorded burial chambers whether it be before or after the fact. To achieve this massive undertaking, architects and engineers alike would tell you that it is impossible to build such monuments with the precision they had, even with today's technology.

Historians have been implementing these beliefs for 4,600 years now. Ancient Egyptians lionized the star Sirius as the giver of life, the star appearing as usual when the annual floods would come from the Nile. When Sirius sank into the west and disappeared from the night sky, it remained hidden for 70 days before surfacing in the east in the morning. This was regarded as a time of ending and renewal. Khemitians never spoke of death but instead they preferred "westing" as Grandma Anta "wested" in Chapter 13 "West in peace".

Khemitians knew that they were essentially immortal and that they were constantly in a state of transformation or change. Many books have been written about Khemit and to me, it is a fascinating topic. As I feed off my natural curiosity, it nourishes me but also baffles me at the same time. Like Liz, I am a seeker of "truths" constantly recreating myself, and with that little fight in me, I just can't help educating myself and others on the subject.

Evidence all over Egypt always comes to pass. As in, the Baghdad battery! *Ahhhhh*, the jar made of earthenware the size of a man's wrist. It is said that its existence could require man to rewrite history altogether! This was also the object Khafa displayed in her council meeting and it caused an uproar and disbelief amongst the Queen's Panel. And just like Khemitology as a whole is usually shunned, so was Khafa and her project. In the ancient temple of Abydos, Egypt, the famous "helicopter" hieroglyphs depicted on the temple walls created such a stir worldwide, especially over the Internet.

If archaeology and science say it has been manipulated or altered, are Egyptian authorities systematically restricting us from the truth? If not, why are scholars being refused access these sites? And here is the thing that throws me off the most—Why are tour guides not allowed to point these out? Is it in the name of protecting science? Or something much larger than life?

Khemit says we are *not* the most advanced we'll ever be, and this takes me back to the explanation of the Baghdad battery. Comfortably basking in the national Museum of Iraq, is our Baghdad battery. One of many found in Egypt, and depicted on various sites, on temple walls. According to history this "voltaic pile" or electricity battery, was invented by Count Alessandro Volta in the 1800. Volta concluded that when two dissimilar metal probes were placed against frog tissue, a weak electric current was generated. The small scale battery in Baghdad indicates that Count Volta didn't invent the battery, but reinvented it!

In 1938, German archeologist Wilhelm Konig, was the first to describe the Baghdad battery. Still today, it is unclear if Konig dug up the object himself, or with the resources of the museum. All we know is that it was found with several others, in Khujut Rabu, on the outskirts of Baghdad. Publishing a paper in 1940, Konig described the jars as being about 2,000 years old, consisting of an earthenware shell and bearing a stopper composed of asphalt. On top of the stopper is an iron rod and lining the inside of the jar is a cylinder of copper. Konig believed these items looked like electric batteries, as stated in his paper.

The inevitable prevention of the follow up on the jars was caused by World War II. But after hostilities ceased, an American by the name of Willard F.M. Gray, who worked at the time for General Electric High Voltage Laboratory in Pittsfield, Massachusetts, worked on the reproduction of the jars. He filled the devices with an electrolyte like grape juice and they had produced about two volts. The battery is widely unaccepted, by science no less.

The suggestion of these devices was one of them being simple jars that held papyrus scrolls which have rotted away in time. A romantic hypothesis is that there is nothing about the batteries that is high tech and the assembly of the jars were common in origin and well within the means of the people of that era. While Alessandro Volta has a place in history that is reassured, in Khemit nothing is sure, according to science. Ancient Megalithic structures were built all over the world, in places such as Tikal, Guatemala, England's famous Stonehenge, and China as well as India.

The Chinese had the same traditions, using the "dragon lines" where monuments were built on electromagnetic fields. Claude Swanson, a well-known physicist, said that over the last 20 years, experiments have been done and they concluded that there is a certain amount of energy at the sites that is unknown to science today. Robert Schoch, PhD and geologist of Boston University, says the idea of the pyramids at Giza being burial chambers is of a "childish nature." For John Burke, a biological engineer, it made sense that all megalithic structures were built because the people had an interest in their population. He also said monuments as such, in different continents of the world, were placed on grounds where an unusual type of geology naturally concentrated the daily magnetic forces. Hakim also confirms that granite, which is a stone found in the great pyramids passageways, is a transmission stone as well as a live stone.

John Burke also concludes that they definitely knew what they were doing in terms of engineering, granite is slightly radioactive and it will ionize or electrify the air. The inside of the great pyramids are not highly decorative like those of the Valley of the Kings, but have rather a more functional decor, indicative of daily use.

Khemit comes across as a new trend of thought for most, and I believe the real mysteries of Egypt lie in Khemit and not in some fictional story like the "Curse of King Tut's tomb," even if it's a good story. Khemit isn't fictional, it was a way of life. It's a mysticism so strong and so righteous that cover ups were inevitable throughout history. Hakim passed away in 2008, leaving behind a legacy for all. It is up to us to understand it fully, to broaden our horizons and to understand that our basic needs for everyday life comes from the very core of the earth.

It's simplicity at its best, divinity before our eyes, and where mankind holds its own destructive hand for money and supreme power. A power our ancients held at no cost to our own. It is preposterous and selfish to think that mankind today has a reached a pivotal point in successfully creating technology. We are light years away from the successes our ancients had, yet we choose to look the other way and claim the mighty prize for ourselves.

The truths of our unlimited potentials have been concealed from us as we navigate a dualistic world of light and dark energies and of feelings of separations from a "God" as well as from each other. Khemit scholars invite all walks of life to combine their efforts with them on a vital mission of hope and great discoveries! My only question is…will we?!